PRINTER'S DEVIL

STONA FITCH

Published by Two Ravens Press Ltd.
Green Willow Croft
Rhiroy
Lochbroom
Ullapool
Ross-shire IV23 2SF

www.tworavenspress.com

The right of Stona Fitch to be identified as author of this work has been asserted by him in accordance with the Copyright, Designs and Patent Act, 1988. © Stona Fitch, 2009.

ISBN: 978-1-906120-32-0

British Library Cataloguing in Publication Data: a CIP record for this book can be obtained from the British Library.

All rights reserved. No part of this publication may be reproduced, stored in a retrieval system, or transmitted in any other form or by any means, electronic, mechanical, photocopying, recording or otherwise without the prior written permission of the publishers. This book may not be lent, hired out, resold or otherwise disposed of by way of trade in any form of binding or cover other than that in which it is published, without the prior consent of the publishers.

Designed and typeset in Sabon by Two Ravens Press.
Cover design by David Knowles and Sharon Blackie.

Printed on Forest Stewardship Council-accredited paper by the MPG Books Group

The publisher gratefully acknowledges subsidy from the Scottish Arts Council towards the publication of this volume.

About the Author

Of Scottish-Cherokee ancestry, Stona Fitch lives in Concord, Massachusetts, with his family. His novels have been published in the U.K., France, Germany, and the U.S. His novel *Senseless* (Two Ravens Press, 2008) is now an independent feature film from Scottish director Simon Hynd. He is the founder of the controversial Concord Free Press, which publishes novels and gives them away for free.

For more information about the author, see
www.tworavenspress.com

Acknowledgements

Endless thanks to Allan Guthrie, Sharon Blackie, and David Knowles. Thanks also to Megan Abbott, Ray Banks, Laura Hynd, Doug Johnstone, and all Two Ravens Press authors (and readers).

For Ann

And in memory of William Kincaid and Gloria Emerson, two teachers of very different lessons

We trained some birds to steal their wheat.
They sent to us exploding ambassadors of peace.
We do this, they do that.
Ten thousand (10,000) years, ten thousand (10,000)
brutal, beautiful years.

— *The People of the Other Village,* Thomas Lux

Invocation

They say ink in the womb darkens our spirits from the very start. Ink leaks from our mothers' breasts and courses through our winding veins. Ink flows from our wounds. But this is a myth of our guild, no more true than any other prop. It's our clever work that stains us. Printing leaves its mark on our fingers; hatred and fear taint our hearts. We know much of damage and little of forgiveness.

How will this latest outside job end? We may be heroes or martyrs, lush or culled. After three days in Shattuck, we will know the end. For now, I'll begin our story armed only with clear eyes and precise words.

May this story be my last.

Friday

Carbon 850 ppm. Yellow conditions prevail all day in urban sectors. Seacoast will experience dioxide fog in the a.m., clearing by noon. Elders, infants, and those with compromised breathing urged to stay settled and oxygenated. Shelters open on an as-needed basis to authorized personnel only.

Start with the three of us walking through the faltering city in close formation, heads down against the wind that waters our eyes and sours our mouths. A yellow day like any other. We walk past elegant buildings, blackened balconies twisted and windows hollow-eyed. Where gardens once bloomed, mosaics of mudcrust stretch out to meet the rutted streets.

Gerry nods toward a brownstone. 'This one.'

Those with cash still settle in the better sectors. But the right address will not protect them. Nothing will.

Gerry pulls a jangling ring of steel pins from his pocket and leans toward the metal door, revealing the landscape of red welts that rim his neck. He pushes two pins into the lock with his thick, darkened fingers and turns. The door clicks open.

Gerry whispers the pressman's litany. '*Precision above all else.*'

We step into a dark entryway and shut the door, closing the city out. I crave silent moments. I want to be free from the howling wind, clattering presses, arguing in small rooms. I want to stay in the dark, quiet doorway forever. But there is work to be done.

'Third floor, on the left,' Gerry says. 'I'm not so sure how this is going to play out. Sean, you stay behind, ready if I need you.'

Sean nods, eager to get started.

'Ian, you try to keep out of the way.'

I know not to take offence. Gerry hasn't survived since the Chaos by being polite. This morning, Gerry called Nils a scrambler right in front of the pressmen and all Nils did was shake his head and smile.

Gerry pulls me close by the shoulders and stares at me with yellowed eyes. 'Ian Greenwald.' His lazy tongue rolls over every letter. 'If your father could see you now, doing an outside job with his guild brothers.'

I shoot Gerry a wither, struggle against his hard grip.

He laughs and lets me go, leads our unlikely band up the stairs. Though Gerry is as heavy as Ian and I combined, he has a thief's grace. He hardly makes a sound as he springs up the old wooden staircase, fingers never touching the railing. At the top, Gerry does his fast work on another lock and the door swings open slowly. Then the hinges let out a long squeal and he rolls his eyes.

'Who is it?' A crimped voice echoes from inside a cavernous apartment. Sean pulls the door closed behind us, careful to touch the knob only with the sleeve of his drabs.

'It's me. Gerry. Just coming to make a deposit, Mr. Sullivan.'

We drift slowly into the living room. A thin man in a dark suit stands up from the head of a long table, napkin tucked jauntily in his collar. The notorious Mr. Sullivan glances at each of us, surprised but not scared. I look at his plate, stacked with pieces of shrivelled corn from the provinces. This is what bankers eat?

'Making a deposit now, afterhours, here? That's bank business, Gerry, you know that.' Sullivan talks to Gerry as if he is slow. He is anything but. 'And just how did you get in here?'

Gerry shrugs. 'Through the post slot? Listen, Sullivan. Nils wants to put this in his deposit box with the rest.' He holds up the black bag. 'Said you should put it in there tonight.'

Sullivan shakes his head and sits down. 'Absolutely not.' He looks the part of banker in his white shirt and dark trousers. No drabs for him. That a crooked banker wouldn't look any different from an honest one never occurred to me.

'Why not?' Gerry asks.

Sullivan shifts in his chair and the light glints off the gold pin in his earlobe. His greying hair is carefully combed back, his face red and cancerous from sailing – paintings of boats line the walls. Sailing is good now, always a wind. A silver cross glimmers above the pictures and our eyes are drawn toward it, scavs seeking metal.

'We're closed for the holiday, of course,' Sullivan says. 'I can make a deposit on Tuesday morning, but that's the earliest.'

'I don't think Nils would like that,' Gerry says. 'It's a lot of cash to leave around here during the long weekend. Wouldn't be right.'

Two glasses stand next to Sullivan's plate. He drinks a careful sip of water, leaves the red wine alone.

'What if we went to your bank right now and you put it in our deposit box? Won't take more than an hour. How about it?' Gerry turns his head to the side and raises his eyebrows. His fingers tighten on the duffelbag's strap.

'Can't do it.' Sullivan takes a deep drink, wine this time. 'Besides, even if I could get into the bank at this hour, something like this would draw attention to our…'

Gerry smiles. 'To our what?'

'Our arrangement.' Sullivan stares at his corn as if trying to figure out how to eat it. But his pale hands stay still on either side of the plate, long fingers stretched out like roots.

'And would you call this arrangement *special*, Mr. Sullivan? Is it a special arrangement?'

'Of course,' he says softly. 'We've been doing business for years now. And I think it's been mutually beneficial.'

'Mutually beneficial,' Gerry says. 'As in we both get something out of it.'

'Exactly. That's exactly it, Gerry.'

I look over at Sean and try to catch his eye, but his gaze is drifting around the apartment. Talk bores him.

Gerry goes on. 'Our cash is safe from the Alliance, easy for us to get to, and you get a cut of everything. What is it now, ten…?'

'Ten percent, yes.'

'And no one knows about it, right? Other people knowing about it would *not* be mutually beneficial, correct?'

'Of course not, Gerry.'

Gerry pauses for a moment. 'You know, in all these years, I never caught your first name, Mr. Sullivan.'

'It's James.'

'James!' Gerry pauses, as if examining each character of the name for flaw, then nods. 'Not Jim. Or Jimmy?'

'James.'

'Could we call you *Jesus*, Mr. Sullivan? Would that be tolerable for you?' Gerry bends down and squints into his duffelbag.

Sean snaps back to attention and turns to watch. Gerry has shifted and we all know it, even Sullivan. The daemonmill in Gerry's mind is turning. His eyes narrow and race. In the pressroom, we know these signals well. They tell us to step far away from Gerry's press.

'No. I take that name rather seriously,' Sullivan says. 'And I'd appreciate it if you would do the same.' The air thickens with threat. I stop breathing and the room swims with floating sparks. I take careful, long draws of stale air.

Sullivan watches Gerry rummage in the duffelbag, wanting to see the cash. I see him at his desk at the bank, counting piles of faded bills. Then again, he probably never puts his pale hands on cash. When you are in charge, you don't have to touch the ingredients, the heavy tools, the base elements. You hover above it all.

'Oh, I take it seriously, all right.' Gerry paces in a tight circle, one hand tucked into the duffelbag. 'The same way I take everything seriously. For example, we've played it straight for what, six years or so, right? Never told anyone about our arrangement. So I must say I was surprised, Mr. Sullivan, when I heard that you mentioned to certain other printers in other sectors ... no names, of course ... that we were putting large amounts of cash in your safe. Even more surprised to find out that you made these other unnamed printers the same mutually beneficial offer, for a fee, of course. So perhaps *Judas* would be more appropriate.'

'I'm sure what you heard wasn't ...'

Instead of cash, Gerry takes out three nails, long ones with wide heads. He rolls them between his thick fingers, black ink lodged in crescents beneath his fingernails, stubbed fingertips stained dead seawater grey. Sean watches closely now. I breathe deeply to keep from verging.

Stop it, Gerry, I think. But I say nothing. As this new job turns down a darker path, all I can do is watch and remember the details. Nils always wants details.

Gerry holds the nails high. '*With three soldiers of steel, I will conquer the world.* Someone said something like that once, Mr. Sullivan. One of us, a printer. He was talking about moveable type, and there were more than three pieces, of course ... in the alphabet ... character set ... not actually steel, lead they were ...' Gerry mumbles on for a moment, mind sputtering into the ditches, then hones in on Sullivan again. 'But I think it applies to our present situation.'

Then Gerry quits talking and grips two nails in the corner of his mouth, takes one in his left hand. Sullivan lurches away from the table but Sean grabs him and clamps his hand tight over Sullivan's thin lips. The banker's eyes widen when Gerry pulls a battered hammer from his duffelbag.

Gerry centres the nail quickly on Sullivan's pale left hand. Without thinking, I step forward to grab Gerry's arm. He turns toward me, hammer held high, and in his burning eyes I see that he would swing at me, Sean, anyone. I step back.

He turns and brings the hammer down with one swift stroke.

Against my instructions to watch and remember everything, I close my eyes and see nothing. I hear the terrible, fleshy thud and Sullivan's half-scream escaping through Sean's fingers. I imagine steel driving through bone and vessel and emerging into wood. It sickens me, proof that I haven't turned cold. But I do nothing to stop it.

The banker is no innocent. But who is now? He is as arrogant and hateful as the other functionaries of the Alliance, the ones Mrs. Boyle calls *l'armée grise*. He is half good and half bad like all of us, just doing his job, never expecting the arrival of three printers, three soldiers of steel.

When I open my eyes, Gerry is kneeling in front of Sullivan, who is trying to pull his hand away from the table but can't.

I want to run as far from this room as fast as I can. This last job is already shifting into a new and darker sector. But if I run, Gerry will follow, swinging his hammer at me, an enemy like any other – or worse, a traitor against the guild.

'I'm not asking you to take away all the sins of the world.' The nails tucked in the corner of Gerry's mouth rise and fall as he mutters, 'I'm just asking you for one important piece of information. Give it to me now and we stop. You wear a bandage for a few weeks and that's that. Or …' Gerry points to his mouth.

What a difference pain makes. Sullivan's cheeks blaze bright red. His mouth is clenched open, thin lips pulled back to reveal wine-brown teeth.

'Stop it. Stop it now,' Sullivan shouts, as if trapped outside on a red day.

'Just tell me the number of the safe deposit box where Sevenheads keeps his cash.'

Sullivan shakes his head quickly. 'I don't know the number. And if I did, I wouldn't tell you.'

Gerry takes the nails from his mouth. 'Oh, you wouldn't tell me? Well, think about it another way, Mr. Jesus Sullivan, crooked banker to the world.' Gerry stalks around the room now, spit flying from his lips as he speaks. A thin trail of sweat gleams on his ulcerous neck. 'It could be someone from Shattuck here right now, asking you the same question about us. And I can bet you that Sevenheads would be a lot less polite about it.'

'Polite?' Sullivan stares wide-eyed at his left hand. A thin rivulet of blood leads from his hand to the edge of the table and drips on the carpet.

Gerry nods toward Sullivan's plate. 'It's only your left hand. You can still eat, can't you? Take a bite. Hate to waste good food. What with rationing and all.'

Sullivan stares at Gerry.

'Help him out, Sean.'

The sound of Sean's name breaks through his haze. Sean probably knows that what we are doing is wrong. But he always does as he's told, which makes him very useful to the guild.

Sean picks up a piece of corn and holds it near the banker's lips. When Sullivan still won't bite, Sean shoves the whole cob in his mouth. Sullivan spits it toward Gerry but it just rolls across the table and tumbles to the floor.

'Fine; same again, then.' Gerry reaches over and pins Sullivan's free arm to the table. I shut my eyes for a moment, hear the hammer's second strike and another choked scream. When I open my eyes, Sullivan's clenched face points toward the ceiling and his thin body makes a palsied dance. Sean wrestles him back down in his chair. He has knocked his wine glass over. Gerry shakes his head, sets the glass gently back on the table.

Gerry taught me how to be a printer. He spent hours explaining how to ink the rollers and keep the paper in register. But the expert pressman is gone now, encased beneath an icy carapace. He has no more sympathy for Sullivan than the black wind has for those it culls. Still, Gerry works with a grace and precision that makes us forget that what he's doing is terribly wrong.

Gerry stalks around the room, nods at the silver cross, then takes it down and tosses it in his duffelbag. 'I'm sure you're familiar with your Gospel.'

Sullivan looks straight ahead.

'Not the Gospel of Lucre, either. The Gospel of Luke. The parable of the Tax Collector and the Pharisee.' Gerry paces a slow circle around the table. His knowledge comes from printing scripture, not reading it. We remember pieces of what runs through our presses.

Sullivan says nothing.

'Two men came to the temple,' Gerry says. 'The first was the Pharisee, a self-righteous wanker who stood by himself and told God how good he had been, about how he fasted and gave money to the church.'

Gerry waits for Sullivan to say something, but his mouth just twists in pain. 'The second man was a tax collector, a dirty, loud guy that everyone hated.' Gerry leans forward and smiles. 'A guy kind of like me, but with more cash.'

No one says anything. In the silence, urgent voices echo from down on the street. Curfew is coming.

'The tax collector just stood there and told God he was a sinner and asked for mercy. He knew what he was doing was wrong. He knew he was a bad man. But he begged. He begged for mercy.'

Eyes shimmering with inexplicable tears, Gerry stops in front of Sullivan and kneels next to him. 'Would you ever ask anyone for mercy?'

Sullivan says nothing.

'Of course you wouldn't. Too proud. Too sure you're a good person,' Gerry mutters. 'The parable ends with a message, and I quote – *All who exalt themselves will be humbled, but all who humble themselves will be exalted.* So I ask you to be humble and give us the number. Please.'

Sullivan stares blankly ahead, lips puffing and blowing in the dusty air of the expensive settle.

'We can leave you alone to think about it,' Gerry offers after a moment.

Sullivan speaks so softly at first that we have to lean forward to hear him. 'There are one thousand and sixty-six deposit boxes at Depositor's Trust,' he says. 'You'll just have to find the one you're looking for.'

'Maybe we will. Not a bad idea at all. But this means days of work for us. And a lot of damage and loss for you and your dirty bank. So a more mutually beneficial solution would be for you to tell us the number right now.'

'I'm not going to tell you anything,' Sullivan says, voice wavering. 'Now or later.'

'That's your choice, then. And in your position, I'd probably do the same. So I respect your decision, your bravery even. I really do.' Gerry walks behind Mr. Sullivan and positions a nail carefully on the top of his head. I close my eyes as Gerry raises the hammer.

Sullivan gives out a short scream before Sean can clamp a hand over his mouth. I open my eyes and see Mr. Sullivan sitting still, mouth open, tongue lolling. I can't see the nail and think for a moment that Gerry has taken pity on him. Then a slow, dark trickle runs down Sullivan's temple and drips from his chin onto his plate. He tries to lift one of his hands to wipe it away.

Gerry bends down and speaks gently. 'Anything you'd like to say, Mr. Sullivan?'

Mr. Sullivan looks toward him and smiles.

'A message ... confession ... number?'

Sullivan opens his mouth but says nothing. Then his eyes roll back a little and he lowers his head slowly to the table, as if he is very tired after a long day at the bank. His cheek rests on a corncob. Gerry reaches out and centres Sullivan's head gently on the plate. The silver head of the nail glimmers like a tiny lost coin in his thin grey hair.

'Good night, sweet Pharisee,' Gerry whispers into Sullivan's ear. Tears stream down Gerry's pockmarked face. Then he wipes them away on the sleeve of his drabs and turns to us, calm now. 'Must have been a little off-centre with the last nail. Usually they last longer than that.'

Sean just shakes his head slowly. I can't even move.

'Ian, I'm sorry. I know you don't like any of this,' Gerry says softly. He has shifted back to become a pressman, a friend of my father. He walks toward me with his thick arms outstretched, puts his hands on my shoulders, works them gently. 'You look like you're about to verge. But it's over now. The rest is easy. You know what they say about bankers, don't you?'

I shake my head. Like all printers, Gerry is a walking codex of apocrypha.

'They say that the real crime isn't robbing a bank, it's founding one. Sullivan was an enemy of the guild. So we had to strike first. A necessary move. Checkmate.' He smiles. We used to play chess during long runs.

I close my eyes to stop the room from spinning. When I open them, I see Sullivan's lips moving slowly, as if he is chewing something small, tough, and bitter – his soul perhaps. Blood pools in his plate and his shallow breathing sends small ripples across the red harbour.

Gerry walks over and grasps Sullivan's earlobe between his fingers, then pulls back quickly. He drops something in my hand. 'A little present for your girl, the scrambler.'

'Melina.' The gold special privileges pin holds a bit of flesh that I brush to the floor. I shiver, drop the pin in my pocket.

Gerry points at Sean. 'Make it look like the opposition did it.'

'What?'

'Write something on the wall.'

'Like what?'

Gerry turns to me. 'You're the teller, you do it.' He points at Sullivan's plate, then the wall.

I think for a moment, then dip my finger in the blood, pretending it's only red ink. *No to their Yes,* I write, then run my finger across the plate again. *Yes to all else.*

Gerry raises his eyebrows. 'A way with words. How about a little more?'

Another dip, then I make the bold, intertwined N and O of the National Opposition.

'Let's go.'

Gerry walks through the apartment, turning over tables, dumping drawers out on the floor. He opens a back bedroom; it's lined with rows of gleaming oxygen tanks.

'Authorized to use any shelter, and he still hoarded.' Gerry shakes his head. 'You know what they say…'

'*Oxygen is theft.*' Sean repeats the slogan that marks so many walls in the city.

'That's right.' Gerry says. '*Air is for all.* Time to set it free.' He wraps his hand in his sleeve, reaches up, and opens each of the nozzles. A choir of hissing valves fills the room. Sean and I step forward and breathe deeply, breathing in the pure, delicious O_2. Oxygen is hope and limitless choices and possibilities. Oxygen is life distilled. We crave it. We want to stand breathing in Sullivan's apartment for hours.

'Enough of that.' Gerry pulls us out, leaving the tanks hissing. 'Don't want you boys to get used to being lush.'

We walk carefully through the apartment and click the door behind us. There is no one on the landing, no neighbour watching from a half-opened door. They are all gone for the weekend. People with cash never stay in the city during holidays. They get out, which is what Mr. Sullivan should have done. Innocents, curfew-breakers, scavs – they die from being in the wrong place at the wrong time. An old story.

○ ● ○

We blend into the crowd shuffling along the wide, ruined street. Back in the Consumption, thieves looked like thieves. They wore black leather or long overcoats. Now we need to stay drab. Strays in word or deed are tagged or cut loose to the howling, unmonitored lands outside the city.

We glance ahead, scanning for Sevenheads and his guild, Alliance smugs with their stoppers. Along the median, dented transports spark along the rails, taking people home for the holiday weekend. There will be parades along the ancient highways, picnics on synth lawns, widespread longing for Retail.

Down the hill, ruined towers tilt by the dry harbour, as if a child's hand has rearranged our ancient city, first a beacon for the ambitious, then the evil. The sun stains the carnelian horizon, pure light filtered through the viscous atmosphere. We have beautiful sunsets now, like endless summer.

We come to a corner building marked with a glowing triangle no bigger than a hand, which holds every walker's gaze.

'Still kind of green, don't you think?' Sean says.

Gerry shakes his head. 'Yellow, definitely on the far end. I don't get this winded unless it's yellow.' He bends over with his hands on his knees for a moment, mouth open, belly heaving as he takes fast draws.

'*Yellow, yellow, chokes a fellow.*' Sean chants the litany of the nursery, the schoolyard.

I add a hopeful note. '*Green day, breathe away.*'

Sean smiles. '*Red, red, you're almost dead.*'

'*Black, black, you won't come back.*' Gerry scratches his pockmarked neck, flicks a speck of himself to the ground. 'Let's go home.'

An elder with a trim white beard stands on the next corner. 'We have opened a hole in the sky with our wickedness,' he shouts to the crowd. 'And now the eye of God watches us through it.'

Gerry rolls his eyes. More than wickedness burned a swirling hole in the sky – the *coryalis*, a delicate name for something so enduring. There are as many descriptions for the coryalis as there are people to watch it – eye of God, deadly vortex, shimmering deceiver, portal to the heavens. I studied atmospherics at the academy and know its real origins – fluorocarbons, oxides of nitrogen, antimony particles, carbon monoxide and its dark brother, CO_2.

'Come on, let's go,' Gerry says.

I hold out my palm. 'Wait.' Nils likes me to listen to these Gnostic meteorologists. What they say might protect us. They are a guild of sorts, one that wanders across all sectors, makes nothing but streetcorner prophecy. The truth comes from alt sources now. All else is prop.

'God sends His pure breath down among us to take us back to Heaven,' he shouts, voice rising higher. 'There is no reason to fear its blessed arrival, brothers and sisters. No reason to cower in shelters.'

Gerry rolls his eyes again. Pure breath, hardly. The black wind is nothing. No oxygen. No life. Nothing. Retreating for a moment to words, always the teller's haven, I note how little separates *breath* from *death*.

The prophet steps forward like a lecturer making his final argument back at the academy. 'Stand tall and await your summons, for each of us will be called and judged. This is the truth from which you cannot hide.' He scans the grey-green clouds, then nods slowly. 'Mark my words. In two days, this sensor will turn black. May we all be among the chosen!'

'No thanks,' Gerry mutters. 'I don't know why you even bother listening to them, Ian,' he says. 'All they do is say the same things over and over. *Eye of God. Pure breath. Await your summons with a smile on your face.*'

'You never know where you'll find wisdom.'

'They're all scrambled, if you ask me,' Gerry says.

'We better hope they are,' Sean says. 'Two days from now we'll be deep in Shattuck, and I don't want to think about the black wind catching us there.'

'Don't verge, Sean. No one's going to catch us,' Gerry says. 'No one. Anyway, the black wind hasn't been back for a long time. They've got it under control.'

'*Sunriser*,' Sean whispers.

We turn into an alley behind a row of abandoned settles, windows billowing with shredded cloth. Sean takes out his bullybar and pops the cover. They crawl down. I pause for a moment, anchor myself against a brick wall with one hand, and look back downtown.

Sean and Gerry can't see me standing still, as if I am at the midpoint of a tightrope and can't decide whether to follow them or stay in the alley. I could leave before our job turns worse. I could blend in with the crowd of drabs trudging home.

Then Sean calls from below and I turn to join them. I have acclimatised – this is one of the strengths and flaws of our guild. We can get used to anything.

I climb down into the hole and lower the cover carefully behind me.

We crouch in a dank underground chamber, once a switching station, the wall lined with broken gauges and brass levers sawed off long ago by scavs, leaving only sharpened stubs. Sean scrapes a flare against the wall and it sizzles to life, lighting our way down the tunnel that heads toward the West End.

We churn the dead air as we walk. Sean holds the sputtering flare and throws gravel into the darkness to keep the grey slurry of skeletal rats moving ahead of us. Flushed and wheezing, Gerry huffs along next to me. He carries the duffelbag loosely, ready to drop it in a second if he has to, but that isn't likely. During our years in the tunnels we have only ever come across a couple of bug-eyed air-wasters, and they were already culled.

Hidden deep beneath the city, we travel down one underground line to another. We hunch in ancient steam vents. We crawl down sewerpipes toward the crusted harbourfloor. As we near Central Station, we turn onto a spur of pipe so narrow that Gerry has to push his bag in front of him with one hand, the gritty soles of his boots scraping along inches from my face. Staying aboveground like good little drabs, we could have crossed most of the city already. But tunnels keep us hidden until we get where we need to go.

We crawl out from a vent onto the station's ruined platform and dust ourselves off. Here our cell of three diverges – Gerry bound for the guildhall, Sean for the pubs, me for Melina's settle.

'Tomorrow, in Shattuck,' Gerry says.

We nod in unison. Tomorrow, in Shattuck.

I stand on the platform and watch their flares disappear down separate tunnels. The cavernous station echoes with the low, distant vibrations of the city. I smell acrid smoke and rotting wood. Tangible shafts of light from the street filter through ducts in the ceiling. I look down at my hands. Like my father before me, I am a foot soldier in an army stained with ink and blood, not all that different in the failing light.

I circle the block where Melina told me I'd find her this week, searching the dusty streets, scanning every door. It's a transitional sector, ideal for the opposition. Most of the windows are dark. Those that are lit flicker as the grid fails and recovers. The warm air smells of woodsmoke and papers blow down the street. When I find copies of the *Sliver*, I know that she can't be far away. If I find Mrs. Boyle, I'll find Melina, her daughter by default.

Across the city wait thousands of empty buildings and abandoned settles. When most people move in, they try to eliminate all traces of the strangers who once lived there. They throw their belongings out into the street to be carted away by scavs. They don't want to be reminded that they live in settles claimed from the culled and disappeared. All Mrs. Boyle does is mark the front door of her provo home with three short, horizontal chalklines. But Mrs. Boyle is no ordinary settler.

I walk quickly down the street, searching for the marked door. If I don't find it soon, I'll have to drop down into the tunnels again and wait until morning. Once I lost Melina for ten panicked days. The city is diminished but still vast, with dozens of sectors where Mrs. Boyle and the opposition might set up.

The metal gratings of the cornershops slam down. A few men wait in entryways, still as stones in the river of drabs that rushes by them. They're unconcerned by the curfew, just minutes away. No doubt they have some sort of nightwork ahead of them. Others stare at the busy street as if it is a puzzle they can't solve. The black wind has marked their mind and scrambled their thoughts. Each one was once like me, capable of walking through the city before curfew, of finding safety in a settle, shelter, or guildhall. They had friends and relatives, lovers who once craved their touch. Now they speak earnestly to empty corners, stare intently up at the sky, as if they could will the wind to bring back what it has taken.

I push gently past. I will do anything for Melina, but can do nothing for these strangers.

When the siren sounds its first blast, I stand on a darkened sidestreet, squinting at the doors. The street is empty save for a circle of glistening crows picking strips of meat from a bloodless rat. Some fear the crows, see them as harbingers of the black wind. But I find them comforting. They are the city's true sensors. As long as crows loiter along the streets, there is enough oxygen.

In the distance, two smugs carry sputtering flares that light the street with a white, unforgiving glow. They walk slowly, one on each side, torches held high, signalling all walkers that it is time to run or risk being reported or tagged. I check a few last doors before I run to a tunnel cover and go underground again.

A door opens and an arm reaches out to grab me and pull me inside. Hands push me down on the floor. I raise my arms to my neck to protect it from a crescent knife.

'I didn't...'

'Quiet,' whispers a voice. 'Let them pass.'

The smugs stalk by, in no hurry. They own the streets now. The flare sends its brutal glow tracing through the entryway, and in it I see one of Mrs. Boyle's volunteers. I don't know his name – there are too many for that. But I recognize his long, dark hair and serious eyes. At the guildhall, they ridicule the opposition's seriousness and idealism. Printers are realists, tethered to the tangible by ink, paper, letters, and words.

We watch the smugs disappear at the far end of the street.

I stand and dust myself off. 'Why didn't you mark the door?'

'We forgot.'

'So how am I supposed to find you, wander around the city and wait until someone grabs me?'

He shrugs. 'I don't know. We'll mark it later.'

'Well, let me know when you do,' I say sharply. Nils always says that this is the real problem with the opposition – they are disorganized and lack precision. With Nils in charge rather than Mrs. Boyle, the Alliance would have been overthrown long ago.

I follow the volunteer up the splintered staircase.

He turns at the top. 'You're late. We've been waiting for you for hours.'

I give him a blank look. 'Had a busy afternoon.' When

I close my eyes I see Mr. Sullivan's head on a plate, his thin lips moving

We walk inside the flat, unnoticed by the crowd. I pass a clump of men huddled together, staring at a large, blank sheet of paper. Mrs. Boyle sits behind a desk, scrawling. She wears a wrinkled white shirt and dark silk pants, plundered, no doubt, from the closets of the culled.

'We're not ready,' she says firmly, without looking up.

'I can wait.' I want to find Melina.

'Don't bother her now,' Mrs. Boyle says, guessing what I'm up to. 'She's texting the last pages.'

I sit next to Mrs. Boyle's desk and watch as her hand moves across the page, inspired by some latest abuse of power by the Alliance. Time, worry, and years of UVR line her face. Her long grey hair is pulled back and clipped hastily in a silver barrette.

After a few minutes, Mrs. Boyle reaches for her glass of wine, eyes never leaving the page. She holds the glass toward me. 'Bordeaux?' she says. 'It's almost as old as I am. But much sweeter and better preserved.'

'No thanks.'

'Shame. The owners – Shaw was their name, put their monogram on everything – the rich are so territorial about their possessions. But these Shaws had remarkable taste, bless their dead souls.' Evidence of the Shaws' former wealth fills the ruined library. A piano, dusty oil paintings of scowling men, fading photos of a family standing along a mountain trail.

Metal desks and crates crowd the centre of the room, a provo office that might last a day, week, month.

She points to the huddle of men across the room.

'See that one at the centre?' Mrs. Boyle whispers. 'The nervous one with the short, black hair?'

I nod. The man stares at a piece of paper while his bleary comrades sputter with laughter.

'He wrote *Air is for all*,' she says reverently.

I nod, wonder what it feels like to write a slogan that everyone in the city knows.

'That was years ago,' she says. 'Hasn't come up with anything that good in a long time.'

'There's still time for inspiration,' I say flatly. I don't love the opposition, just Melina.

She shakes her head. 'They'll be tagged soon enough, the devils.' She rubs the black metal stud in her earlobe and sees me watching her. 'They used these to catch thieves, did you know that? At Retail, of course, during the Consumption. I found that out just the other day. That's where tagging came from. People who ran the shops put these on expensive clothes. They set off alarms if people walked out without paying.' She laughs at this ridiculous collection of ideas – expensive clothes, thieves who would bother stealing them, trying to protect something so unimportant.

I say nothing. Her black tag bans Mrs. Boyle from any shelter. She will be left outside on red or black days. Being tagged gives her great credibility among the opposition, but will cull her in the end.

'Technology never goes wanting for a new way to be misused. History proves me out on this point.' Mrs. Boyle turns toward me. 'But you don't care anything about history or politics, do you? You and the patchwork girl. You're just heathens living for the present, aren't you? Fucking like there's no tomorrow. And maybe you're right; that's the sad part. Maybe there really isn't a tomorrow.'

I shrug. 'Tomorrow is Saturday.' I think of our job in Shattuck.

'You could get tagged just for being with us in this room, you know. Or for running our press.' She points at her pages, frowns at a phrase, crosses it out.

I look around the room. For all its clever slogans and night marches, the opposition looks about as dangerous as my childhood teachers teaching me the four Cs. They leave the violence to the scavs, thieves, and printers.

'I'm here because you pay me,' I say. It's only half true. Melina holds a more powerful attraction than any amount of cash.

Mrs. Boyle thrusts out the stack of pages. 'Take my latest brilliant issuances slash effluences up to her. She's waiting on the top floor.'

I reach out my hand, fingers still stained red.

Mrs. Boyle sees it too, detects a trace of this afternoon's work in my eyes. She grabs my blood-speckled sleeve and pulls me close.

'Those printers will steal your soul if you let them,' she hisses. 'They're charming and brutal. But you know that.'

I nod. 'Yes, I know that.'

She lets me go. 'Just be careful, for God's sake. And one more thing…'

I turn at the doorway.

'Please don't fuck her until she's done with her work,' Mrs. Boyle shouts. Everyone else in the room quits talking and turns to listen. 'We're on a deadline. And you know how muddled she gets after.'

I shoot her a wither and walk upstairs.

I joined the opposition by accident. Sean and I were working third shift, printing thousands of sector-transfer forms for the Alliance. The press hummed at top speed, its feeder full of fresh stock. Say what you will about the Alliance, but it's been good for printing. Power means paperwork – enough forms to keep our guild lush.

Sean and I were sleeping like dogs in a pile of scrap paper. I woke and saw two strangers standing next to the ink shelves – a pale, weathered, serious woman with a beautiful, silent girl at her side. Mother and daughter, a case of opposites.

Mrs. Boyle's sharp glance took in the clutter of the pressroom. She eyed the press clattering away unattended, the aluminium plates hanging up to dry, proof pages pinned on the wall. Melina kept one hand on Mrs. Boyle's shoulder and I thought for a moment that she might be blind.

Mrs. Boyle's lips were moving, though I couldn't hear her over the roar of the press. I would find out later that talking was Mrs. Boyle's natural state, even if no one paid attention. She was a fount of wisdom, or at least words – and enough words might add up to wisdom.

I shut off the press and Sean stirred, rubbing his eyes. 'Problem?' While we slept, the plate sometimes wore out, or the feeder might malfunction and send paper raining down on us.

I pointed. 'Visitors.'

'…and it doesn't have to be a big press. In fact, it must be mobile.'

Sean squinted. 'Who are you?'

'We want to buy a press,' Mrs. Boyle said firmly.

'It's illegal to own a press,' I said. 'Unless you're a printer.'

'Of course, I know that, you idiot,' Mrs. Boyle hissed. 'Why would I be here, after curfew, in the hideous West End, carrying this?' She held up a dainty little leather case and opened its clasps to reveal stacks of cash. 'Your guild has a reputation for being … highly negotiable.'

I smiled and nodded toward the door to the offices. Sean rubbed his eyes and wandered upstairs to find Nils, who never seemed to sleep. He was always interested in parting strangers from their cash.

We stood in silence for a moment. Mrs. Boyle waited to talk to someone more important than a printer's devil sleeping through the third shift. I was stilled by Melina's beauty, made more fascinating because of her damage. Melina shifted from side to side, smiled at a passing thought. Her left eye was cloudy and pulled down at the corner. The left side of her mouth barely moved, leaving her smile crooked.

Every few moments, she lurched slightly to one side. Mrs. Boyle reached out to catch her, comfort her.

'What do you want to print?' I asked finally to fill the silence.

'The truth,' Mrs. Boyle shot back. And I believed her.

I pause for a second at the door, watching Melina texting at a tiny desk in a cluttered attic room. I have printed dozens of issues of the *Sliver* and spent countless nights in Mrs. Boyle's provo settles across the city. But I am still learning to decipher Melina. Our time together is always brief. Mrs. Boyle keeps us both busy and rarely leaves us alone. Despite this, Melina and I have made love on blankets, shattered parquet floors, ancient furniture. Desire always finds a way.

Melina doesn't look up when I walk in. She's focused on her work, turning Mrs. Boyle's scrawled words into this week's issue.

Originally, Mrs. Boyle called her opposition newspaper the *Silver Star*, a hopeful reference to a day when the atmosphere might thin enough to let us see a star again. But Melina transposed the letters and the *Sliver* was born. Mrs. Boyle liked it better, penned the tagline – *A Sliver of Hope in a Hopeless Time*.

Melina might be texting something about the Alliance and its abuses, how innocents were tagged for simply questioning regulations. It might be about how thousands of scientists and researchers couldn't seem to shrink the coryalis. There were suspicions that the Alliance controlled the black wind, directed it to undesirable sectors. Or the article might be about the rich bankers and Alliance cronies – *l'armée grise*

– all living in comfort and safety while others struggled. Or it might be about the barbaric elitism of special privileges, how the shelters should be open to everyone. *Oxygen is theft. Air is for all.*

Whatever the article, its meaning will be lost on Melina. She sees only letters and words, punctuation and spaces. Melina knows order but not meaning. Mrs. Boyle's words mean no more than a scrap of paper she might find blowing down the street. Among all the damage that the black wind did to her, this is the saving grace, the sliver of hope. She is open to all messages.

I put Mrs. Boyle's article on the board in front of Melina and she squints at the scrawled words, scrawled with such anger that the pen has torn the paper.

When she comes to the end of a page, Melina turns and looks up, giving me a crooked smile.

I kiss her on the forehead, just once, not wanting to go further and set off Mrs. Boyle's legendary temper. I watch Melina work on the final page, fingers hovering over the metal keys, eyes rarely straying from the blue screen. She can set type like no one I have ever seen before, texting the copy, building the columns, setting initial capitals, and checking line endings. Creating order on the page helps her sort the disorder in her mind. Melina once described her thoughts as a room full of children, all screaming for attention. A dream she had of walking through a field was as real as seeing me sitting on the dusty couch.

The question from my guild brothers sticks with me – why love someone who is damaged? If I thought they might understand it, I would explain that character resides in defects and scars. We are all damaged, senses annealed, thoughts gone cold – this is how we survive. Melina's damage is simply more visible.

Melina finishes and presses a key. The final page comes out of the back of the screen and rolls onto the desk. She folds the keyboard and screen together and puts them in the metal case, then slides the case into her backpack. She moves with the focus and concentration of someone who knows that the machine she handles is important, dangerous even.

When I see Melina at work, it's hard not to think that she could be cured by the right words in a precise order, delivered at the right time. In my dreams I make the patchwork girl whole again, cure her body and mind. For a moment I understand why Mrs. Boyle keeps going on – tagged, reviled and chased from one settle to the next. Why fight unless there is hope?

Everyone in the city hopes that the black wind will fade and the coryalis will close like a tired eye. Until then, we rely on our delusions – faith to protect us, suspicion to keep us safe, love to lead us on.

Melina walks toward me, her dragging leg marking slack lines along the dusty floor. I am ashamed of the wave of disappointment that passes through me when I see Melina's damage. It's wrong to expect her to be any different.

She sits on the couch next to me and pushes her finger deep into my mouth, touching one tooth and then another, counting. Then she touches her own front teeth.

'This one's loose,' she insists. 'They told me at the shelter it might fall out next week if I eat hard bread.' The tooth fell out more than a decade ago. Her mind dwells on the time of her parents' martyrdom.

She shifts closer to me and looks to the corners of the room. 'There are rats here, you know that? We have to keep the barrels closed up tight.' She jerks suddenly to the right and almost falls, but I catch her, feel the warmth of her arm beneath a worn grey sweater.

'I know that,' I say. 'I've seen them.'

'Mrs. Boyle told me about a rat that played the flute, a story that made the people laugh, about everyone following like rats. Do you think people are like that, all following along?'

She stands and holds my hands gently in hers, eyes staring

intently into mine, as if we are about to begin an elaborate dance from an earlier time.

'A quadrille,' she says, divining my thought. The damage left her eye opaque, but her mind is open, aware and receiving. 'I read about it once. Ladies danced to golden violins…' She drops my hands and laughs, forgetting about the dance. 'A message!' She picks up the page she has just finished and frowns at it, hands it to me. 'It's in Latin. I speak it, you know.'

'Do you?'

'Ian taught me. *Terra voluptatis*. The pleasure lands. He's going to take me there someday with cash and oxygen and…'

I kiss her on the forehead. 'I'm Ian.'

She frowns, throws her arms around my neck. 'Aren't you supposed to be in the shelter? It's a red day.'

'Yellow, just yellow.'

'*Yellow, yellow, chokes a fellow.*' She tilts her head from side to side, then stops and blinks. 'That last page, where is it?'

I hold up the metal roll, embossed with thousands of letters.

She turns serious and clear. 'You need to print it, Ian. They're waiting. Then come back up after everyone's gone.'

'What are you going to do?'

'I'm going to sleep for a little bit. I'm tired and my eyes hurt…' She stretches out on the couch. Giving my hand one last touch, she curls into a ball and closes her eyes.

I pull a red blanket up to her waist and kiss her on the cheek, then make my way through the cluttered room.

'Don't turn the light off,' she whispers. 'Tell everyone I love them very much. All of them. Even the serious ones.'

Melina looks so much like her mother at that moment that I can picture Vanessa Lamartine, arms crossed as she stands in front of the locked shelter. I know her only from Mrs. Boyle's prop films. I see the Lamartines in their long leather jackets, the black wind curling invisibly around them, Melina at their feet. I close the door softly, leaving Melina to shuffle through her unsorted thoughts and memories, stringing them like beads only to untie them again.

Downstairs, I walk unnoticed through the crowded living room, where the best minds in the opposition are opening dusty bottles of wine and taking deep pulls. Mrs. Boyle sits at her desk, scribbling again. She is always broadcasting some kind of message. Even in silence, words seem to hover around her like sparks.

I find the press in the corner, carefully set up on a low table and loaded with paper, a stack of aluminium plates next to it. Jason perches on a stool reading his frayed copy of *History of the Chaos,* a revisionist account that the Alliance had banned – as much a revolutionary accessory as his black tag.

He jumps up when he sees me. 'We're ready.'

I nod and hand him the last page, then check the press. I fill the fountain solution and click the inking rollers into place.

Jason stands close to the press, as fascinated by it as I am. Disassembled, the mobile press fits within a small backpack. The days when engineers could design a press so compact and brilliant are over. Inside Mrs. Boyle's press, the mechanical tolerances grow with each run and the motors throw off more heat degree by degree. The machinery's fatal drifting is ramping up slowly. One day, friction will send a spark into the motor's oiled coils, the press will smoulder and burn, and there will be nothing I can do to stop it.

For now, I print and try not to think about the future. I am in the opposition settle, printing the *Sliver,* marking time until I can go back up to see Melina.

I mount a test plate on the press and turn the cylinders on to start inking. Political theory, plans for resistance, slogans meant to unite the scattered opposition – these all pale beside the beautiful efficiency of the press in motion. Radicals and patriots put the words together but printers send them out into the world. We are inexorably linked. But while we can live without them, they can't live without us. At least, this is the prop we tell ourselves.

Every printer uses some meaningless type to check the press before a run. Sometimes they print the alphabet. Others have favourite sayings or passages. For years, Gerry printed same line over and over – *Every Good Boy Desires Cash*. He found this phrase as amusing as it was crass.

My first sheet coils through the press and comes out next to Jason, who picks it up and reads the familiar words:

> *After Consumption came Convergence,*
> *When Two became Three.*
> *After Chaos came Control,*
> *To set the world Free.*

He rolls his eyes. 'Why do you always print that?'

'Because I need to see whether I have the ink settings right.' I take the sheet from Jason and examine it carefully through a type magnifier, see that the outer edges of the letters are crisp, the inner hollows are open and clear.

'I know that, but why that particular text? *The Four Cs*. It's just prop that the Alliance forces children to learn in schools.'

'Exactly.' The rhyme is from *An Approved History for Young Learners*, a primer the Alliance wrote. My father printed the first edition when I was a child. I remembered him handing me the sheet, black ink glistening, words crisp and sleek in their sans serif font. He told me that even lies had to be printed with precision.

'And you think that's good?'

'No.' Like my father, I find *The Four Cs* ridiculous.

'Well, it's unfair to teach children prop.' Jason gives a self-righteous shake of his thick head.

Mrs. Boyle would enjoy the irony of the little scrap of text that my father liked to print. She would respect my decision to keep it flowing from the press before every job – a memorial, an invocation. Jason is too literal and dull. He wads up the test page and throws it into the corner of the settle.

I clamp the first plate of the *Sliver* into place. The others in the room look up when the low hum and click of the press begins. Then they turn back to their drinking, girding themselves for when it's time to break curfew and deliver thick stacks of papers across the city. I watch the gears mesh, the drive belt tracing an infinite loop.

As always, the drumbeat pulse of the press summons up thoughts of my father. My eyes cloud up suddenly. I turn away from Jason so that he can't see my glistening tears, from an overwhelming sadness that I can't keep at bay. The beautiful press seems to be clicking off the days, one after the next, until I join my father on the Martyrs' Wall.

I shake my head at the foolishness of shedding tears for a machine. But I know that my own days of precision and grace will stop someday as I age, fall apart, host a tumour, choke – whatever lies ahead. For a moment, I wish that I could fool myself the way the sunrisers do. *The sun is rising. It's a new day dawning. The world is healed.*

I wipe my eyes with a rag then ratchet up the paper. I turn the feeder on and the cover of the *Sliver* starts to stack up at the other end of the press. My sadness disappears in the rhythm of the cylinders, the snap of paper. I adjust the ink and water balance levers to keep the type crisp and pure.

The loader at the front of the press empties its paper in a few minutes. I jog new paper stock (scaved from an Alliance press run), load it, and prepare to turn it into opposition prop. Paper never takes sides; it's ready to accept any version of the truth. As Jason carries the finished sheets over to a drying table, I mount the second plate, wipe the rollers clean with a rag, and start the next page.

What would my father say about this tiny press and the black-and-white broadside pages of the *Sliver*? Like all printers, he printed any job for anyone. He printed the Alliance's forms and took its cash. He forged documents and sold them to the opposition. His speciality was filigreed labels for oxygen canisters. The guild did a good business selling canisters of ordinary air as oxygen, bringing false hope to the desperate – a lucrative trade in any era, but one particularly suited for the Chaos and its aftermath. We called our false oxygen *the deadly antidote*, since it killed rather than cured. If anyone discovered the deception, they weren't around to report it.

No matter what the job, my father printed in high resolution, captured all the details, kept every page in perfect registration. Control was his currency. He fought uncertainty with quality, danger with audacity. Watching him behind the press was an education in concentration and obsession. My work will always be its pale shadow.

I finish the next page and Jason carries the stack to the finishing table, where other volunteers wait to cut and collate the pages. As I lock on the next plate, Jason skulks to the back of the press and lifts his long hair, turning his head so that I can see the intertwined *N* and *O* tattooed on the back of his neck.

'That must hurt.' I run my finger along the black lines, the flesh puckered and red around the letters, a rogue display font with painful serifs.

Jason shakes his head. 'Worth it.' He drops his hair back over the tattoo, barely concealing it. 'You get one of these, the women are all over you,' he whispers. 'The rebel. The outlaw. The revolutionary. You get to fuck a lot.'

'That's what they say.' I wipe down the plate, ratchet up the paper. I had read Jason's articles; they weren't very good.

'Not that you need any help. You and Melina are a popular

topic of conversation around here.' He raises his thick eyebrows. 'If you do it with her when she's acting like she's ten years old, do you think that would qualify as child…'

Jason rests his pale hands on the top of the cylinders. I reverse the press suddenly to pull his fingers in. Jason screams and the press sends out a loud squeal as it tries to pull his hand deep into its workings. A larger press would have taken his arm off. A colder man would have let it.

'Sorry, sorry,' Jason shouts. The others look up for a moment, then go back to drinking.

I reverse the press again and his inky hand emerges from the rollers, one fingertip oozing and dark. He shakes his hand and hops up and down like a child who has touched a candle.

Jason's eyes narrow. 'Mrs. Boyle's right about you and your guild. You're a bunch of heathens.'

I shrug. 'Never say anything about Melina. Ever.'

'Okay, okay.' Jason bandages his finger with a rag, giving him a battle-scarred look that might increase his narrow appeal.

Jason stays at the far end of the press for the rest of the run, staring at me pleadingly every now and then like a kicked dog. I say nothing, make no apology. Our guild relies on speed and transformation. We live in the era of *hyper-evolution,* as the academy scientists call it. Fast minds and hands have always been the printer's strength. So we survive.

In an hour, the stacked pages wait on the table and a line of unsteady revolutionaries bind each edition together with string. When the table is empty, they divide the copies of the *Sliver* and hide them in their backpacks. As they leave the apartment, they walk by Mrs. Boyle, who kisses them on both cheeks. Every few weeks, one will fail to come back, detained or culled. It's not a good time to violate curfew. It's a time for staying underground.

The opposition wants to be free from the constraints of the Alliance.

Printers only want to be free to steal, cheat, and profit from the Alliance.

Unlike my hardened brothers at the guildhall, I have a hidden faith. Even in the swirling coryalis, I find beauty and order. But my faith wavers daily with my status within the guild, the nearness of Melina, the quality of the air.

At the academy, the main lesson I learned was how vague and uninformed I was. I conflated memories of my father with my invisible God to create an Omnipotent Printer, reams of wisdom spinning from a celestial press. He still works away in the darkened corner of my mind, enters my idle thoughts with the rhythm of paper passing between cylinders of steel.

I clean the press and break it down into components, then fit them together into a small cube that slides neatly into the green backpack. Mrs. Boyle sits at her desk, asleep with her pen still in hand. Her head sways gently and her eyes twitch beneath her eyelids. I walk past her and carefully climb the stairs, trying not to make a sound. The dry, splintered wood creaks like the deck of an ancient ship.

Melina sleeps on the couch. She curls inward like the letter C. I lie down next to her, pressing close to her warm back. She stirs and turns, smiling, to kiss me, her eyes wide open.

She lurches and I hold her.

'I have to tell you something.' I stare into her dark eyes.

'Yes, of course. Are you finished?'

'Done.'

'Where are the others?'

'They're gone for a bit. Delivering.'

'Good.' Melina smiles and pulls off her sweater. Her skin glows in the dim light, revealing the familiar constellations of moles and scars on a pale sky. I touch her warm breasts and burnish the pale areolas with my rough fingers, lips, tongue.

She reaches out to unbutton my shirt.

I stop and touch her hand. 'You have to listen.'

She takes off my shirt and presses her cheek to my narrow chest. 'Yes? Yes, Ian.'

I reach out to take her hands and place her warm fingertips over my heart. 'Text what I'm saying.' It's the only way I can be sure that she'll remember.

She nods and closes her eyes.

'On Monday morning, I need you to meet me here at Mrs. Boyle's.'

Her fingers move quickly on my chest to tap out the letters, words, the spaces between them. She presses her eyes closed in concentration.

'I'll have the cash and papers we need to go north.'

She smiles. '*Terra voluptatis.*'

The pleasure lands. I invented them long ago to give Melina hope. A sector where the black wind never goes. I patched this mythic place together from descriptions of prairies I read in history books. In truth, the north is unmonitored, given over to farms and the occasional renegade settler. Rumours claim that this sector is safe now, and I believe them. We need hope and a destination.

'I'm doing one last job this weekend...'

Her eyes snap open. 'What kind of...?'

'Something for Nils.'

Melina shakes her head. 'No, that's not right.'

'It'll be fine.'

'Nothing too bad?'

'Printing the *Sliver* is more dangerous, believe me.'

Her gaze goes slightly out of focus. 'The true patriot must write a new future for our land, beneath and between the Alliance's lines of control...' I recognize Mrs. Boyle's editorial from this week's edition. Words catch in Melina's mind like burrs.

I move her hands back to my chest. 'This next part is

important.'

She nods, fingertips poised. I smile for a moment at her seriousness.

'Be ready to leave in a hurry.' I speak slowly, clearly. 'Have all your things in a backpack. Monday morning at nine. Dress for a long trip. And wear this.' I reach into my pocket and drop the gold Special Privileges pin into her palm. Her fingers curl around it.

Her eyes widen as she turns the pin over and over in her hand like a rare jewel. 'Where did you get this?'

'Found it.' Mr. Sullivan didn't need protection any more. In the end, it did him no good. People seldom know their real enemies.

'What about Mrs. Boyle?'

'I'll talk to her.'

'Are we leaving forever?'

'Maybe.'

She bites her lip. 'Good. I like forever.' Melina bends over and kisses me on the lips.

She raises her dress slowly, her thin legs marked with bruises from tables and doorways. She reaches over to unbuckle my drabs and pull them down. We manoeuvre clumsily to eliminate any breath of air between us. Melina rises up and then down to take me inside her in one graceful motion.

I lie back on the couch and watch her pressing down against me furiously, her dark hair swaying back and forth, breasts gently rising and falling, eyes closed. She is beautiful, beautiful and damaged. I reach out to touch her lightly with my darkened fingers.

Melina puts her hands on my chest again and they tap out an insistent message.

'What are you saying?' I whisper.

'That I want you. That I want you to be safe.'

'I am. Now. Here with you.' I push against her, feel her warmth around me.

'I mean all the time, forever.'

I say nothing, remember Gerry's hammer and three soldiers of steel.

'*Terra voluptatis*,' she whispers, smiling, then presses hard against me and holds still, her mouth open and eyes shut. This stolen moment brings tears to my eyes. In this cluttered attic, with curfew falling across the dark city, it is still possible to escape, our bodies pulsing and our thoughts set free. We journey to the pleasure lands, if only for a moment. It is enough.

○ ● ○

I try to slip unnoticed past Mrs. Boyle, but her eyes open slightly at the sound of my steps. 'Leaving so soon, printer?' she says.

'It's late.'

'It's always late.' She reaches out for her glass and takes a long drink of wine. 'Here in the end-time.'

'That's just prop.' I shake my head.

'So what are you, a *sunriser*?' Mrs. Boyle hisses. 'Alliance programmes moving ahead. Coryalis getting smaller every day. Black wind not coming back?'

'Hardly.'

'Believe me, the end is coming, my friend. It's just taking a little longer than we thought.' Mrs. Boyle smiles. 'But what do you care? You're young and free. You have your heathen friends to protect you. Everything seems rosy when you're in love, even when the air around you is killing you, when the Alliance is plotting against you even as we speak…'

'I…' The speech I rehearsed is nowhere to be found. Mrs. Boyle has pushed it into hiding.

Her dark eyes narrow. 'You're leaving with the girl, aren't you?'

'Yes.'

'I knew it.' She slaps the table and the wine bottle jumps.
'How?'
'You don't escape the Alliance for more than a decade without a finely tuned intuition, my dear boy.'
'Are you angry?'
Mrs. Boyle shook her head. 'Of course. Melina needs a great deal of care and patience. You're careless and impatient. You'll have to do more than fuck her. You'll have to take care of her. And that can be a tough go, Ian.'
'I know that.'
'And you're ready to be responsible for her? All the time?'
'Yes.'
'You'll need to be like a parent to her sometimes. To give her strength.'
Mrs. Boyle has the connections reversed. Melina gives me strength. 'I'll be a better parent to her than her own were,' I say.
'You can't judge what they did. It was a statement.'
'Not a very clear one.' Mrs. Boyle is well aware of my opinion of Melina's parents, the legendary, revolutionary Lamartines.
'You know nothing about it.'
'I do, though.'
'Only what I told you.' Mrs. Boyle described their fall to me, as she had to hundreds of recruits, to prove the Alliance's heartlessness.
'My father printed the famous poster of the Lamartine family, standing outside a shelter, arms crossed as the black wind killed them.' I still see shreds of it on walls throughout the city.
'They killed themselves. *Biocide,* they called it.' Mrs. Boyle shrugs. 'As a means of protest, it didn't really take hold. Too extreme.'
'That was their choice. She didn't have one. She was a child

sitting at their feet, wondering what was happening. That she survived at all is amazing.'

'Then you'll have to make up for all the horrible things that have happened to her. Help her forget her childhood and her selfish parents. Isn't that what lovers do for each other? Certainly being around me hasn't helped.'

'I'm hoping she could be reoxygenated. There are new treatments now.'

'That's very expensive.'

'I'm hoping to have some cash soon.'

'And I'm sure that these funds will be coming from your hard-earned wages as an honest printer of Alliance forms, am I right?'

I say nothing.

'I sincerely hope your criminal days are almost behind you, my dear boy. You don't seem cut out for a career in it.'

'So what do you suggest I do?'

'Cook in a provo restaurant and read Dante at night, the patchwork girl by your side, awaiting better times.'

'There aren't many restaurants any more. Dante's depressing, don't you think?'

'Work for the scientific commission, then, tinkering with the air. You did well at the academy. Top of your class, weren't you?'

'Yes. For what it's worth.'

'It could be worth a lot if you let it. Instead of wasting your intelligence on running a press, much as we appreciate it, of course.' Mrs. Boyle shuffles through the papers on her desk, feigning a search for a lost page.

'I like to print,' I say. 'It's in my blood. Besides, thousands of scientists don't seem to be making much progress on the air.'

'Then just what are you going to do?'

A pause. 'Take care of her.'

'That's all?'

'It's enough for me.'

'Then you're a romantic, as well as a heathen and a criminal. And that's not a winning combination. Melina's parents were romantic fools too, and look what happened to them.'

'I wouldn't do anything like that.'

'Make sure that you don't. She's had enough damage.'

'I'll be back on Monday.'

'We'll still be here, I suppose.' She shrugs. 'I like this settle. No one knows we're here. There's still a lot of wine down in the cellar.' She picks up her glass and drains it.

'Goodbye, Mrs. Boyle.'

She raises her hand in a dismissive wave and turns quickly around in her chair, facing the dim, empty room, strewn with backpacks, bottles, crumpled pages of the *Sliver*. As I back out of the room, tears stream down her pale face and drip from her chin. She pushes them away with a furious swipe of her hand and then laughs long and hard.

The curfew emptied the darkened streets of this sector. Good little drabs sleep in safe settles under windswept darkness. Made anonymous by nightfall, I shift from alley to alley. Skulking down the dusty streets, I could be a rat, a bomb-thrower, an air-waster waiting to be culled, anyone.

I pass the Union Street sensor, still bright yellow. I am young enough that yellow can't choke me outright. But if I run more than a block, I'll be wheezing like an elder. If I find myself on the wrong street at the wrong time, I might tumble to the ground like the Lamartines, choking away the slow minutes. The sensors can only detect so much. When it makes one of its rare visits, the black wind grasps deeply into the city. There are stories of friends standing together, only to have one suddenly drop to the ground, culled. Maps of the black wind's progress, drawn by Gnostic meteorologists, are popular at the cornershops. But we need more than maps and predictions.

We have lived with the black wind for decades. Our fear never diminishes, just melds with the wind until they become one.

Mrs. Boyle would argue that we have become like sheep, cream-coloured lumps awaiting inevitable slaughter. But we are not all so docile, so willing to push our throats forward to receive the crescent knife.

In the distance, a smug treads slowly down his appointed route, the wind whipping his dark coat behind him. He comes closer, his bright flare lighting the way. I run into an alley that cuts through to the entrance to Central Station, hiding behind an ancient grey column pitted by gunfire, the volute scrolls at the top havening tired crows.

I hide behind the column, but the crows rise up in a loud, inky cloud that draws the smug's flare closer.

The smug looks down at me, curled at the base of the column like a dog. Heart pounding, I wait for the stopper's pulse.

'Ian?'

I open my eyes, recognize a face from the academy: a student I once knew, though not well. His name comes to me. 'Keith,' I say. 'Keith Solis.' I stand slowly.

We watch each other warily, as men do, placing each other on the continuum of friend to foe. Once we shared top prize in a history class, and Keith let me know that he alone deserved the honour. In a vague way, I remember that he is not to be trusted. An *operator*, he would have been called, in a time when there was much more to operate.

'I didn't know you'd gone into government,' I say finally, breaking the silence.

'Right after the academy. Two years now,' Keith says proudly. His face has thickened and he has adopted a much older voice, as if pretending to be an elder. 'One more year and I'm off the streets. Working at headquarters.'

'Congratulations.' I say it with as much sincerity as I can. 'And you?'

'Working for the printer's guild. In the West End – I'm from there, you know.'

'Oh. A good guild, I've heard. Everyone speaks highly of it.'

Of course they do. Nils cultivates a strong connection with the Alliance, knowing that we need it to survive. In the flarelight I see Keith eyeing my stained drabs, my dirty hair flailing in the wind. He smiles to himself, glad he made the wise decision to stay out of the guilds and keep his hands clean.

He looks around to make sure we are alone, then moves a step closer. 'We're doing great things, you know. Projects you probably haven't even heard about.'

'I'm sure.' I say nothing more, not wanting to reveal what I do or don't know. My time with Mrs. Boyle has given me more than enough insights into the secret workings of the Alliance.

'There are major opportunities opening up and we're taking them,' he says. 'Have you heard of *mendelization?*'

'No.'

'We're saving the strong, culling the weak,' he whispers. 'We can accomplish in decades what used to take generations.' Keith gives an awestruck smile. 'Can you imagine?'

I can. The black wind never seems to cull the rich. The dead on the streets are always cornershop owners, children, scramblers. There's never a grey Alliance uniform sprawled among the choked.

'So what they say is true, then? That you can control the wind?' I want to know – this is the question everyone wants to have answered.

Keith shakes his head. 'Of course not. It's beyond our control. Believe me, if we could, we would. We have hundreds of scientists working on it. But given that we can't, we're making the best of it – taking advantage of a situation, so to speak.'

'A situation?'

'The black wind is a phenomenon – naturally occurring – but we're turning it into a movement, a chance to jump several generations ahead. We're trimming away the heavy burden that slows us down.'

'And that would be…'

'The poor, of course. And the less intelligent, the unskilled, the scramblers. We're in a period of hyper-evolution, Ian. Remember, from the academy?'

'But we caused it by tinkering with the air, adding too much carbon, CFCs, all the rest of it,' I say. 'Maybe *we're* the burden. All of us.'

'Don't be naïve.' Keith looks up at the sky. 'If the world wanted all of us gone, we would be out in a flash. This is just a reduction of the flock. We want to make damn sure we're the ones left when the black wind clears out.'

'We? You mean the Alliance, then?'

Keith nods. 'The Alliance, the guilds we favour, the sectors that seem most likely to help us achieve our mission.'

'Which is?'

Keith gives me an incredulous look – could I be the same student who graduated at the top of our class? 'The same as everyone else's, of course – to survive.'

Keith turns avuncular. He puts his hand on my shoulder to pass along some insights to me, his less-fortunate, dim schoolmate. 'It's really very simple, Ian. There's not enough any more. Not enough air. Not enough rations. Not enough of anything. There never really was, though people liked to pretend there was. Now we can't pretend. We have to protect our friends. Given the choice, that's what anyone would do.'

I nod, remember the Special Privileges pin Gerry plucked from Sullivan's ear. From the moment Gerry dropped the pin in my hand, I wanted nothing more than to give it to Melina and protect her. Being guilty of the same favouritism as the Alliance causes a painful shift in my mind.

'To protect someone takes cash and privileges,' Keith says. 'Love, hope, words – they don't work any more.'

If I ever heard a colder statement, I don't remember it. Keith isn't alone. There are thousands like him, a generation of hard-eyed survivors. There isn't an evil leader behind the Alliance, no Sevenheads at the helm, just a grey army of passionless functionaries protecting each other.

In the distance, a door slams and voices echo down the streets. Keith turns to look and I think of running. The shouts fade and Keith turns to me.

'We can get it all back, you know.' A reverence enters Keith's voice, as if he is speaking of heaven.

'What?'

'The Consumption. The good life. Retail. Oil-burners. Resource-intensive activities. All of it. We just have to be strong and patient.'

I nod, not in agreement, but in the hope that it might send Keith on his way.

'Now I need you to be strong too, for a moment.' Keith looks around the deserted streets. 'I'm being supervised – they're always watching, you know. You violated curfew. I could take you in just for that. You could be tagged.'

I nod.

'I can't just let you go or I'd be reprimanded.' He unsheathes his stopper. 'I'll set it low. But better to clench your teeth a bit so you don't bite off your tongue.'

He points the stopper at my upper leg and presses a button. Nothing happens.

He shakes his head. 'It's old. Sometimes it takes a bit to warm up, sorry.' He presses the button again and the stopper buzzes loudly.

Before I can move, a heavy hand descends and paralyses

me. I stare distractedly at the blue spark that connects the end of the stopper to my leg, shaking now. The pain comes from a place within my body that I know little of. The stopper is drilling a new channel through my bones. I would scream, but my face locks in a rictus, teeth grinding together until I feel the chips on my tongue.

The moment seems long as an hour, then the blue spark stops and I collapse to the ground. Keith sheathes his stopper, leans down to where I sprawl at the station's entrance.

Keith's frozen face shines in the flarelight. 'I'll be looking out for you,' he says, a threat or a promise – I can't tell. Then he walks on, continuing on his appointed circuit through the darkened city, bringing order and pain wherever he goes. The cruel of any era always find their calling.

I try to stand but my leg is numb and weak and pulses with pain. The stopper scrambles me for a moment, makes me unsure of how long I have been here, where I was earlier. I stare up at the words carved along the top of the station – a Latin phrase I know but can't decipher now. The backs of my arms bristle. I close my eyes and wait for my mind to clear.

I retrace my route across the city – from home to the guildhall to Mr. Sullivan's apartment to Mrs. Boyle's settle to the station. I think about our job for Nils. In these details, my thoughts come into focus like type through a magnifier. My leg begins to tingle, the pain fading. I rise slowly, as if from a long illness, and stumble toward the station. Its windows are carefully boarded up, but as Gerry taught us, there is always a way in.

A narrow alley skirts the side of the station. Scraping the dusty ground with my boot, I uncover the circular cover, pop it open quickly with my bullybar, and climb down. The way is so familiar that I don't need a flare. I reach up to drag the cover back in place before I descend the corroded rungs.

At the bottom, I swing a ventilator grate open and crawl out on the platform. I take a flare from my pack and scrape it on the ground. The sputtering light reveals the station platform, piled high with wooden benches tipped over in a maze left behind by whatever event cleared the station years ago. Lycine gas, fire, an exploding suitcase, disease delivered by a wandering child – the escalating assaults and counter-assaults of the Chaos. These struggles seem quaint now. What war can you wage on the wind, on the hole in the sky that lets it in?

It's long after midnight and my feet drag as I cross the station, where Sean and Gerry and I went our separate ways just a few hours ago. Our cell of three will be in Shattuck all weekend, though I would much rather spend it walking the harbourfloor with Melina, helping my mother back at her settle, printing thousands of forms – anything else. The only reward is the cash that lures us on, lots of cash, enough to take Melina out of the city.

When I pass the pile of benches it shifts a little, wood scraping on stone. Something moves beneath the benches. I back away slowly toward the grate, ready to climb back up to the empty square.

Sean rises from the tangle of splintered wood, a bleary phoenix in wrinkled drabs. 'Was sleeping.' He rubs his eyes with his fingers.

'Good. Good for you.'

Sean squints at me, his face splotchy. 'Too bright.'

'Sorry.' I lower the flare. 'Not such a good place to sleep, don't you think?'

'Couldn't help it. You were late.'

'I thought we made a plan to meet up later at the safe-house.'

Sean walks closer. 'I was scared,' he whispers. 'I figured I'd wait here and we'd go together.'

'Fine.'

Sean bends over and picks up a browning newspaper. 'We used to collect these, remember?' He drops the paper back on the ground.

I nod. As boys, we explored the dank, branching tunnels of Central Station until our flares dimmed and we had to climb back up. Along the tracks, we once found a bundle of rotten wallets emptied of cash, a dog skeleton, stacks of ancient cell phones fused together – all the fascinating, worthless artefacts that boys collect and mothers throw away.

The ceiling is marked by congealed drips and rust and holes where chunks of plaster fell. We can still decipher an ancient mural of painted stars and boats and ocean waves.

'That's my favourite part.' I point at a section that shows the square crowded with people rushing down sidewalks. They wear raincoats, dresses, business suits. They carry parcels and leather cases with handles.

Sean squints. 'What is it?'

'That's what the square used to look like.' I stare at the mural. Though each walker is different (the Consumption glorified the individual, after all) they seem to share a sense of purpose. They are walking toward a meeting or appointment and moving fast to get there on time. This mundane urgency is missing from our city. We have honed our diverse ambitions to a narrow point – to keep breathing.

Sean shrugs. 'Looks crowded to me.'

'I like it.' Above us waits the same square, a sensor planted in its dismal centre, surrounded by a bleakscape of seared buildings. 'Back before the Convergence, there was something called *bustle*. A crowd was bustling. People walked fast without getting winded. No one worried about the air.'

'Fools.'

'Maybe.'

'Anyway, they wrecked it all for us.'

'They had no idea.' At the top of the mural, a man stands in a window looking down at the crowd below. His hands curve on the sill as if he has just closed the window to keep out the noise and dirt, then stopped to take one last look before he drew the blinds. I passed through the station so many times, for so many years, that this stranger in the window seems as familiar as a friend.

Sean grabs my sleeve. 'Enough sightseeing, Ian. We've got to get going.'

We walk down the tunnel.

'You're limping.'

'I tripped.' If I tell Sean about my reunion with Keith it will only send him aboveground in search of revenge.

In a few minutes, we leave the West End behind, along with the guildhall and our families. My mother knows that we aren't printing a long run of forms during a holiday weekend. She must suspect that we're doing an outside job for Nils.

But she said nothing, her fears balanced by Nils' kindness. In the years since my father joined the Martyrs' Wall, Nils paid my mother his full salary every week and made sure that our family had extra ration booklets. But she is also well aware that Nils demands allegiance, that his outside jobs take us far from home.

This weekend, I plan to pay back all that I owe the guild. I'll be able to leave without guilt, without a glance back at the West End. Then Melina and I will be free.

We walk in near-darkness, passing under the city's heart and heading toward Shattuck, its dangerous imagination. We leave the subway tunnel and climb into a storm sewer, its walls dry and dusty now, floor lined with rocks that Sean gathers and tosses in front of us. The tunnel narrows and connects to a cement conduit barely big enough for crawling. We get down on our hands and knees and peer into the shaft.

'I don't like this,' Sean mutters. 'Spooks me to be inside something this small.'

'Just crawl. We're not in this one for long.' I roll a flare ahead with one hand, and we inch forward on our knees and elbows.

'I'm serious, Ian,' Sean says. 'I'm about to verge.'

'No you're not.' My face passes so close to the floor of the shaft that I can smell the sour cement and dusty rot.

'I am.'

'Quit wasting air.'

We scrape along in silence until we come to a wider section of tunnel. Sean stands up quickly, dusts off his drabs with his hands. 'I'm getting too old for this.'

'We're the youngest in the guild.'

'And the thinnest, luckily.'

I laugh. We climb a rusted ladder up an airshaft that leads up to Division Street.

Sean pushes up the cover with his bullybar and squints. 'Looks okay,' he whispers.

We climb out into a narrow alley behind a restaurant. Grey-green clouds cling low over the dark streets, lit only by flickering lamps. Hours after curfew, the city air is thick with the smell of frying, floating out of every cornershop, every settle window – the smell of being poor. Sean squints into the wind, his thick hair blowing back.

'I'm hungry,' Sean says. If we surfaced near a rushing stream, he would have been thirsty. He always wants whatever is around. 'Let's stop and get some food.'

I shake my head. 'Everything's closed.'

'There's probably some afterhours place around here. This is Shattuck. They don't care about curfew.'

'The last thing we need is someone seeing us here. We're supposed to just get in and get out.'

'What about this?' He points to a tiny arrow chalked on the sidewalk. We follow it to another arrow so small that it's almost invisible in the dim light. We trace this arrow to the front door of a cornershop.

'It's closed,' I say.

Sean smiles and points to a narrow metal slot. 'Always a way in.' He opens the slot and drops a handful of coins noiselessly into an unseen hand. The door opens a sliver.

'What is it?' The voice isn't friendly, but it isn't angry either.

'We're hungry,' Sean whispers. 'Thirsty, too.'

'Do you have cash?'

Sean pushes some bills through the slot. A thick arm shoots out and pulls him inside, then me. The door slams closed.

We stand in a darkened entryway lit by a distant, flickering bulb. A thin old man in drabs sits on a stool and pushes his pale face at us.

'Let me see you.' He stares for a moment. His skin is lined as parchment, eyes kind but limned in red, as if he never sleeps. Both of his earlobes are missing.

Sean and I look at each other.

'In a guild, are you?'

Sean starts to speak but my lie comes out first. 'At the academy.'

'Shouldn't you be at home studying, young friends?'

'It's a holiday,' I say.

'All right, then. But no trouble from either of you.' He gives us a gentle shove down the hallway.

'He was tagged,' Sean whispers.

'Think so?'

'Then he just cut them off.' Sean shivers. 'Must have hurt.'

'Better than being left outside on a black day and culled.'

'They catch you cutting off your earlobes, they just find other places to put them. Places that really hurt. That's what I've heard.'

'I'm sure it's true.'

We come to a chalk circle on the floor and pull up on a metal handle, raising a wooden hatch. Then we climb down a short tunnel not that different from those we've just crawled down, except that it leads to a large, dim room full of people sitting at tables, drinking and eating.

We sit down at a smaller table in the corner. The room

holds a hushed excitement, as if all those gathered here are conspiring. A few dark-eyed men look up to take note of us, then they go back to their dinners. Their low murmurs blend to become the subterranean voice of the city. An ancient poem I read at the academy described life as *a brief song between two infinite silences.* The city's defiant melody still lingers in dim cellars beneath the grid of dusty streets.

Our table is carved with initials and dates, guild litanies, opposition slogans. Sean picks up a knife from the table and starts to cut into the wood.

I shake my head and he puts down the knife.

A thin waitress with tired eyes and a blue kerchief over her thin hair comes over carrying a skillet full of fried onions and potatoes. We both nod and put a coin in her dark hand. Without a word, she serves us each three careful spoonfuls. The waitress holds up a pitcher and we both nod again, Sean with more enthusiasm. She pours us glasses of beer and takes our coins. Sean, pressing another gently into her hand, lets his fingers stray over her palm for a moment. The waitress smiles at Sean, always the charmer, then moves on to the next table.

'She gave me a look,' Sean says.

'Of course she did. If she didn't look, your potatoes would have ended up on the floor.'

'No, I mean a different kind of look.'

Sean turns in his chair to search for the waitress. I push my fork into a small potato and raise it to check the glistening black strings of limp onions for maggots. No doubt the potatoes were pulled from contaminated soil. The butter is stolen and rancid, beer brewed in a rusted metal barrel in the alley. But what can possibly taste better at midnight?

Sean gives up looking for the waitress. As he eats, he presses his eyes closed in ecstasy. 'This is the best place in the world,' he says. 'I told you it would be.'

I eat ravenously, glad to be alive and to have escaped Keith with only a sore leg.

Sean points at his chest. 'You may know a lot from books and all, but I'm the one who knows his way around.'

I nod. It's true. Sean can smell smugs a sector away, knows every tunnel from Shattuck to the harbourfloor.

We eat and drink in silence, each taking a second serving. Sean presses another coin in the waitress' palm and she closes her hand gently around his fingers for a moment this time, smiling.

I see a dark-bearded man at the long table staring at us with bleary eyes that glint in the half-darkness – from curiosity, anger, or beer. I can't tell.

The waitress moves on and I shoot Sean a wither. 'Stop it. People are watching.'

He smiles. 'Just looking for a little love, Ian. Is that so bad? Maybe I'll try to get her to come back with us tonight.'

'And maybe she'd like to come with us tomorrow too?' I whisper. 'When we rob her sector's bank and steal its guild's cash?'

'Despite what everyone says, the women in Shattuck are beautiful,' Sean says. 'The food here is good too. We should be very happy.'

Sean takes his pleasures where he can find them, a voluptuary in an austere era. A whiff of oxygen. A furtive kiss from a pressman's wife. I have much to learn from him. But as we huddle over our dark table, I can also see the brown half-circle over Sean's left eye where a fist connected, the front tooth chipped by a smug's nightstick. Sean raises his beer and drinks slowly, eyes closed, throat working to quench what I know to be an insatiable thirst.

During the Consumption, people thought more about eating and drinking than breathing and surviving. We joke about it now, shake our heads at all the choices they had – the cuisines, restaurants, dishes. In my dreams, I travel back to ancient bakeries lined with bread and cakes, where

Melina and I spend hours hovering with our forks, picking our way through glistening tarts and layer cakes and runny pies. Melina's body turns plush and curved and I rub my hand along her full belly and heavy breasts. I bite into her shoulder and find her pale skin flaky with white flour, her cherry-red flesh delicious.

We all have these gluttonous dreams of Retail, whether we admit to them or not. But we need to stay hungry, Mrs. Boyle always insists – as if we have a choice.

I sense someone watching us and turn to find the bleary stranger is still staring, as if trying to place us. He raises his glass to his beerslick lips and I see that ink stains his fingers black.

'Don't look now, but there's a printer at the long table,' I say.

Sean puts down his fork and reaches suddenly for the knife and tightens his fingers around it.

'Not a good idea.' I shake my head. 'I think he's drunk. Let's just start on our way.'

We stand slowly and walk out the door. Behind us, chairs scrape on the floor and voices shout. Sean and I climb up and open the hatch, then close it behind us. We set one leg of a heavy bench carefully on top of the hatch, then glide quickly down the narrow entryway.

The guard smiles at us. 'Have a good dinner, young scholars?'

We nod. Sean hands him a coin with none of the careful delivery he applied to the waitress' pay. Behind us, the bench rises and topples with a crash.

'Stop them!' someone shouts. 'They're printers!'

We push out to the street, heedless of any smugs or night watchers who might see us. We run as fast as we can, arms pumping, boots clicking on the hardened dirt.

Sean closes his eyes for a moment as we run and his pace slows. I can hear voices behind us.

'They'll kill us if they catch us, Sean, settle and run.'

He nods. 'Just tell me where we're going.'

'Not sure.'

'They still behind us?'

'Probably.'

All of Shattuck races by like a fever dream. The cornershops become flattened blocks with bare brick chimneys rising into the low sky where the opalescent coryalis swirls. We cross into a part of Shattuck that I don't recognize, each block more destroyed than the last.

When we see the square rising before us we stop in a darkened lot and rest, hands on our knees, chests heaving. After a moment, we look up.

'This isn't good.' Sean covers his eyes with one hand but I can't help staring.

'Why not?'

'Everyone from our guild who has seen this dies, Ian. Twenty people on the Martyrs' Wall, maybe more, saw this and died.'

'It's just a square, Sean. Look at it.'

Sean opens his eyes slowly. We stare at the spectacle before us. An enormous metal letter S, many stories high, rises from the centre of the square.

'Sevenheads,' Sean says with a mix of fear and reverence. His monument is constructed of discarded printing plates, overlapping like thousands of fish scales. We can see sparks from welders dripping to the ground.

Sean points. 'Like nests.' Its two curled interior spaces are large enough to house dozens of tacked-together wooden shelters. Smoke rises from the shacks that have found a provo home there like ravens on a cliffside.

'People find a way to live almost anywhere. I guess they figure Sevenheads will protect them.'

'I don't think so.' Sean studies the monument with a practised eye that travels up the curves and back again. 'Serifs,' he mutters, then laughs.

'Yes, they use serifs.' I can just see them at the beginning and end of the serpentine *S*, sharp corners that end the graceful curve.

Sean shakes his head. 'Big mistake.'

'They would say otherwise.'

'They also use ragged right margins,' Sean shouts. 'We justify our margins.'

'Of course,' I say. 'So we can print government forms.'

'And Sevenheads can't hold a hard edge. Ever seen a hairline rule printed in Shattuck? It's all wrong, no precision.'

'I believe you.'

'Do you, Ian?'

'Yes.'

Sean stops shouting, settles. 'Do you think seeing this will cull us?'

I shrug. 'There are worse things to see than an enormous letter.' I know that this monument represents much more. It's Sevenheads in typographic form, much more tolerable in metal than in the flesh. We can only hope that we never see that alt version that breathes, that hates all rival printers from the West End.

'We have to get away from here.' Sean grabs my shoulder and we run away from the enormous sparking *S*. It shrinks in point size from headline to subhead to boldface to body copy to agate. But it is still the same *S*, the sign of Sevenheads, our enemy, who prints heedlessly in serif fonts, margins unjustified, on cheap paper stock made from weeds dissolved in lye.

A letter, a monument, a portent – we run from it.

Crows rustle along the roof of the safehouse at the end of a darkened street. Either the power grid is out or everyone is asleep. I can't say. Shattuck isn't a popular settle – too dangerous and far from any shelter.

'Got the key?' Sean asks, though he knows I do. Gerry may be our leader, but Nils gives me all the instructions, since I listen and remember.

We walk up the stairs, shimmering with broken glass. I match the key's number to a number carved on a thick door and open it. The light from my flare shows that the room is nearly empty – two narrow cots line the wooden floor and two duffelbags wait next to them. They are black and almost big enough to hold a body: mine, Sean's, or another.

Sean starts to open one of the duffelbags.

'That's for tomorrow,' I say.

Sean turns to the boxes that line the wall and finds flares, oxygen tanks, stacks of cash, a case of bullybars.

'Everything a thief could ask for,' I say.

'Except something to drink.'

'Haven't you had enough?'

'It's hard to shake Gerry's hammer job on that guy. Don't want to dream about it.'

'Me neither.' I stub out the flare and lie back on the cot, trying to fill my mind with Melina alone. My thoughts trace the slow line of her cheekbone. So much of her life has been spent hiding that she seems to be of another, paler, furtive species, one that…

'…to Shattuck?' Sean says from his cot.

'What?'

'Where were you, Ian? Thinking about your friend…?'

'Melina.'

'Ought to bring her around the guildhall more. I don't care what the others say…'

I turn. 'So what do they say?'

'That you shouldn't waste your time with someone that … you know.'

'No, Sean. I don't have a glimmer. What do you mean?'

'You know. Life's short. Real short. Why waste time on a

scrambler? Particularly from the opposition. She'll be tagged in no time, hanging out with that crazy one who bought the press from us.'

'Mrs. Boyle?'

'Yeah, that loud one. All that talk'll get her in trouble, mark my words.'

'She's tagged already, what else could happen?'

'They'll just put a stopper on her heart – you know they'd like to, Ian. I seen them do it. Someone gets a little wise on the street and that's all. Plenty of good people have had a stopper put to their hearts...'

'What are you so nervous about?'

'What?'

'Got a bad feeling about this job?'

Sean and I have known each other for so long that even sitting in the dark, in a safehouse in Shattuck, I can picture his expression as he thinks through my question – his thick eyebrows bunching together, mouth working.

'Yeah, I guess I do.'

I do too, though I don't say it.

'I hate it when Gerry goes mental like that,' he says. 'I thought Sevenheads was supposed to be the crazy one.'

I shiver in the dark, though the air in the room is hot and still. 'Sevenheads is worse, believe me.'

'How come everyone's so scared of Sevenheads? I could just take him out.' Sean jumps out of his cot and grabs a bullybar. He does a quick spin around the room, dropping to his knees and aiming at an imaginary enemy lurking in the corners. More than anything, he wants a stopper.

'Too late for that,' I say.

Sean leans the bullybar against the door so that it will topple over if anyone moves it, then tumbles heavily on his cot. 'That's why Nils picked us for this job, you know. Because we're tougher than Sevenheads.'

'Don't fool yourself. He picked us because we're dispensable.'

'What?'

'We're not that important to the guild. Just a step up from apprentices.'

Sean turns quiet for a moment. 'Don't be so sure about that, Ian. You're his favourite. I seen the way Nils is around you, all friendly, talking about old times and your father.'

'That's just the way he is. He makes everyone feel like they're special – that's how he gets them to do what he wants.'

'Tell me about the old days, Ian.'

'You know about them already.' I'm used to Sean's requests for stories and recitations of the guild's litanies. This is a teller's work. But tonight I just want to stay quiet.

Sean puts his hands under his head and closes his eyes. 'Tell me something that will help me sleep.'

I pause and try to come up with the right story. 'Back during the Chaos, there was a printer named Sorenson. He ran a big six-colour press, the biggest one in the shop. He stood at the back next to the controls and ran it as fast as he could. Eight-up aluminium plates as big as tables flew on, flew off. Ink was splashing everywhere. The press was smoking when he finished a run. One day an apprentice, Kirk – I didn't know him – got his sleeve caught in the works and Sorenson didn't even stop, just ran him all the way through the –'

'I've heard this one. It's just a story they tell to scare new apprentices.'

'It happened, Sean.' I saw the press after the accident, its cylinders bloodied and bent, clots of hair and cloth clinging to the plate. The apprentice's path through the press was preserved on a hundred sheets of fine rag stock, his tragic story printed in his own fluids. I gathered with the others and watched the pressmen wiping down the cylinders, knowing full well it could have been any of us. We were all just tender sacks of ink waiting to stain the page.

'Then what happened?'

'Nils shut the presses down for a week and pushed Sorenson out the door to spend some time dodging the black wind. This was serious punishment. Back then, the sirens went off almost every night. Some sector or another was always getting choked. Sorenson was out there alone.'

'You must have been hoping he wouldn't come back.'

I nod. 'We all hoped he'd get culled.' We wanted our hatred to mark him and bring revenge down on him. But the black wind is perverse. How could it be drawn to an innocent like Melina but not to Sorenson, legendary for cruelty? This was my mistake – giving the wind volition when it has none. Barren of oxygen, the black wind is also emptied of desire. It just travels on its wayward path, innocent and deadly as a contagious child.

'But he came back, right?'

'And he wasn't alone.' I pause. 'You sure you want to hear this part? I'm not sure it's going to help you sleep.'

'He's just someone everyone's decided to be scared of,' Sean says sharply. 'Like the Devil or the Alliance smugs. He's just a printer like anyone else.'

'But after he came back, he was different.'

'How?'

'He brought back a woman he met on the streets,' I say. 'A thin, dark woman with a tear tattooed under each eye and something written on her hands in a language we couldn't decipher.'

'Why did he bring her in?'

I shrug. Why did we bring anyone in? Because even during the Chaos, there was still empathy and kindness. 'Anyway, after she arrived, Sorenson built a kind of cage around his press. They took their meals alone, stayed away from guild meetings, never stood sentry duty.'

'What was he doing?'

'Printing. We'd just leave plates next to the door and he'd put out the finished jobs in the morning. You'd catch a glimpse of his woman wandering through the pressroom. When she spoke it sounded like birds screeching. You'd see Sorenson working late at night. Pale as paper. His hands were enormous, big as tunnel covers.'

'You were a kid then. Everything just looked bigger.'

I shake my head. 'He was big, believe me. Then one day he came running out of his pressroom. His woman was having a baby. No one even knew she was pregnant. All the guild women ran into the pressroom. They were in there all day. We heard shouting for hours and hours, then screaming. No work got done. The presses were idle. We all just wandered around waiting for it to end. And late that night, it did.'

'She almost died, right?' Sean's voice is quiet and thick with sleep.

'Yes. She gave birth to a son, full-term and dead. And this is the part no one likes to talk about. He had extra heads, small and without eyes, the necks no thicker than fingers. Seven in all. On that day, Sorenson, one of our best printers, became Sevenheads, our guild's rival.'

Sean exhales loudly.

'There were a lot of poisons then, mutagens, runoff. Worse than now, even. It was inevitable.' I saw Sevenheads' dead child, a lump of flesh in a bowl of crimson haemorrhage, its neck fringed with blind heads. From that moment, the stillborn hydra lurked in my dreams, its eyes waiting for a signal to open. I know that one day they will.

Sean says nothing.

I keep telling the story. 'People in our sector weren't even supposed to have children. The Alliance had a regulation about it. Most couldn't even conceive. But Sevenheads and his wife learned the hard way that this wasn't time to bring a child into the city, though he blamed Nils for it. Said our inks did it, that they were toxic. That night, he cleaned out their cage, wheeled out their possessions, and left.'

I look over at Sean. His lips move as if he's trying to speak but he is asleep, lulled by the story of Sevenheads, the same one apprentices still tell each other to inspire nightmares. *Don't go out at night or Sevenheads will run you through his press…*

I reach over and pull Sean's blanket up to his chin, watch his face ripple with dreams. Asleep, he still looks peaceful and young, not all that different from the way he looked back in school. The darkness hides the early grey hair among the black, the scars on his face. Everyone loves Sean, our favourite, a charmer who can do no wrong – smiling as if the world is fine and pure.

Through the window, I can see the low orange surge of methane lightning, faraway and silent. It comes from the north, where Melina and I hope to be in just a few days. There is always a way in, as Gerry tells us all the time. But we are looking for a way out.

On the night Sevenheads defected, I found Nils on the roof of the guildhall, watching fire ripple across the upper atmosphere. He gave no sign of anger at being betrayed by one of his own printers. With shooting stars hidden behind layers of clouds, we watched the sky smoulder instead. On warm nights when the sensors turned green, all the apprentices would bring blankets up and sleep huddled on the roof, our pale faces lit by the distant burning, the fires decades in the making, even slower to be extinguished. They were beautiful.

Nils stood alone on the roof. As I walked toward him, he had already registered my footsteps, identified me as the walker, and decided what to say. Through the hard years, Nils was all things to everyone in the guild: our best friend, father, confidante, confessor, protector, and negotiator. We knew no other leader and wanted none. He turned as I walked closer and reached his hand down.

Without saying anything, I tapped his hand and waited for his fingers to open. I was a child, still expecting all surprises to be good. He unfurled his clenched fingers and a small lead soldier fell into my waiting palm.

'Sevenheads made it,' Nils said. 'We found them in his shop.'

I turned the soldier over in my hand. It was crude and quickly poured. The type hadn't heated completely and I could still make out letters along the soldier's legs and arms. There were buckets of stray lead type in the guildhall waiting to be melted into something useful.

Nils noticed how I studied the letters. 'He was always in a hurry. Now he can hurry to a new sector and leave us to live in peace. Though I doubt that will be the case.' He gripped my shoulder gently with his inky fingers.

'I need everyone to be a soldier now,' he said. 'We all have to fight together or we will all die together. It's certain.'

I nodded without knowing why, agreeing simply because he asked me to. Nils had a way of making us all feel like we were part of an inseparable family, like we could count on each other no matter how hard or dangerous the job might be.

'Will you be a soldier for me, Ian?'

I nodded again. What did an angry boy, robbed of his father and childhood by the Chaos, want to do – except fight?

He bent low, his grey eyes connecting with mine. 'Some soldiers fight with weapons. But I want you to use something else.'

I said nothing.

'I've watched you. You sense things that other people don't. You notice the details – missing type on a proof, the way the crows leave before the wind turns black.'

I couldn't deny it. We had lived in such close quarters for so long that everyone's strengths and weaknesses were known to Nils.

'You have a gift.'

I blushed at being singled out. Apprentices were always striving to catch Nils' eye by printing faster than the next or taking on extra shifts.

'And I want you to put it to work for the good of the guild. To be our teller, the one who watches, learns the litanies, spreads our glory. Would you do this?'

I didn't hesitate. 'Yes.'

Nils bent down, his grey eyes locked with mine as he said the printer's litany I had heard so many times before. *'We live by our wits, our work, and our willingness to do anything to survive. Precision above all else. This is the word of the guild.'*

'This is the word of the guild,' I repeated, thankful to be entrusted. This was the guild that my father had died for. But I also knew that if it weren't for the guild, he wouldn't have died. In this way, my loyalty was split even then between the guild and my own intuition – the quiet voice of my own mind that spoke to me in the darkness at night while the other apprentices slept. I grew to trust this voice more and more and to resist the easy camaraderie of my guild brothers, the fleeting rewards of cash. But more than a dozen years later, I am still a guild foot-soldier, heading out to battle.

Here in an empty building deep in the heart of Shattuck, Sean and I wait for tomorrow's job to start. I lie down to sleep, hoping to dream of Melina and a transport heading north, far away from Nils, Gerry, Sevenheads, and the rest. In the ancient times, dreams came through two gates – a marble gate for dreams that might come true, a gate of horn for those that were false dreams, intended only to lead the dreamer astray. I hope that my dreams come through the marble gate, but like so much else, it isn't up to me.

○ ● ○

The nightmare appears, summoned up by tonight's talk of Sevenheads and my worries about tomorrow's work. It moves with the urgency of a battle postponed. Sevenheads chases me along a path of coarse stones, gaining every moment, my faltering steps no match for his long strides. The path is uneven and tangled. I glance down quickly to see my feet stepping along the tops of letters, words, sentences – then realize that I am running across the story I am telling. If I tell it right, I can run faster and escape.

Each word poses new challenges. *Running* is low and linear, with only the capital *R* and hovering dot over the letter *i* to squeeze under. The letters are made of pumice or rough stone that scrapes my skin bloodslick if I have to climb them. And *climb* is difficult, a dead-stop *l* followed by a hovering *i*, then three steps across *m* to face a second vertice on the *b*, slowing me and giving Sevenheads time to close in.

I have to revise my story to suit my needs, like any teller. I make the sentences sleek, with few verticals to scrape my skin. Some words are so streamlined that they seem made for running – *convergence, crows, escape...*

I write quickly, the low words keeping me ahead of Sevenheads. The teller's role isn't always to amuse and pass the slow hours on press. There is much more to it than that. I have to tell my story as if my survival depends on it.

○ ● ○

I wake in the safehouse, skin sweating, mind lost among words, revealed for what they are, traps for the unwary. Across the room, Sean sleeps quietly, breath going in, oxygen fuelling his own dreams, simpler and less dangerous than mine, I hope.

Running away and telling the story as I run – my nightmare is obvious; all dreams are distillations (a terrifying word to climb, with its forest of verticals). When the job is over, I will run far away, but first I have to tell the story. I am ready to run from all demons, to set new type in my mind.

My father stayed and fought, earning only a place on the

Martyrs' Wall. There is nothing I can do but run from it all. Run and tell the story – this is always the teller's trade, in ancient times and in dreams.

Saturday

Carbon 970 ppm. Yellow conditions in the morning and afternoon, giving way to atmospheric inversion at sunset. Toxicity heavy at times, with red conditions possible in western sectors. Shelters open on an as-needed basis to authorized personnel. Curfew strictly enforced during holiday weekend.

The streets of Shattuck are still dark when Sean and I wake and silently pack our things, shuffling around the dim settle like scramblers on a streetcorner. We carry the duffelbags down an alley behind Center Street, stealing slowly toward Shattuck Square, eyes open wide, hands on our bullybars, as if they would save us.

The sky brightens to the east, the whorl of the coryalis nearly overhead. A few exhaust fans are already running in the bakeries and cafés, pushing the smell of frying into the alley. Threadbare rats sweep ahead in a brown tide.

Sean shakes his head, pulls his cap low. 'You see rats moving around in the morning, it's real bad. I read that somewhere.'

'If they're moving around it's because they're hungry, like us. Don't get spooked already.'

Sean stops in the alley and grabs my shoulder. 'I'm serious, Ian. I got a bad feeling about this. A really bad feeling. Like today's going to go black or something. Let's just quit right now and go home.'

'And what are you going to tell Gerry? Or Nils?'

'Just tell them it's all my fault. They can lock me up or kick me out of the guild or whatever they do. I don't care.' He drops his duffelbag and walks back down the alley.

'Knock it off, Sean. You know we've got to do this. You said it yourself last night. You said you were a hard one, ready for anything. And now you're walking away from this? We're cut in, remember. Ten percent.'

Sean stops. 'Of what?'

'Of whatever.'

'Could be nothing, you know. Could be a stopper to the heart.'

'Could be lush, too. Gerry said so.'

Sean stands for a moment, moving his mouth, looking around the alley as if the answer waits somewhere along its shabby fringes. 'I'll do it,' he says finally. 'But this is my last job for Nils. I swear.'

'You say that every time.' I don't mention that it is my last job for him as well. If Sean found out about my plan, he would try to convince me to stay.

'I mean it this time. I really do, Ian. I'm getting too old for this.'

'Right.' We walk down the alley, lugging our duffels. Further down, almost in the square, we come to the back entrance of an office, its sign showing a smiling mouth with a ray of light reflecting from one tooth. I wonder why scavs didn't take this sign and burn it years ago. It wouldn't have lasted a minute in our sector.

'What are we supposed to do, stand around here until the smugs come?' I check my watch. It is almost six. When I look up, Gerry is standing under the sign.

'You waiting to see the dentist? I know I am.' Gerry smiles, showing his blackened teeth, snarled into impossible angles. Gerry waves us over to the back door and we stand behind him as he peers into the narrow window, its glass broken, protected only by thin metal bars. Gerry takes a bar in each hand and pulls them apart, face reddening. After a moment, the metal begins to bend until Gerry can reach his gloved hand inside.

Gerry turns the deadbolt and we slip quickly inside the dark office. He bends the bars back, leaving only a small glint on the rusted steel to mark our arrival.

I light a flare and hold it up to reveal an ancient office, desks overturned, walls marked with craters. A thick layer of dust covers the room like ashes. At the centre of the main room waits a simple wooden chair with rotten leather straps dangling from its arms.

We walk inside the office. The stale air hangs, tangible and amniotic, over the scattered furniture. No one has been here since the Chaos. I kick at a grey pyramid next to the chair and break a layer of dust to reveal hundreds of teeth, roots brown and crusted, crowns broken to scav the gold. I don't want to know any more about this office or its terrible history.

Gerry waves us down a hallway to a small cubicle, its floor thick with mildewed papers.

'This is the spot.' He looks me in the eye. 'Ian. You take a look outside the front door every couple of minutes and make sure no one is in the alley. Sean, you open up the bags and get the gear ready to go.' Gerry's eyes dart around as he speaks, and he has the same intensity as he did yesterday at Mr. Sullivan's apartment, as if he is thinking of hundreds of details at once.

'I'm going to tap into the grid so we can run this stuff.' Gerry walks into a back room and Sean unzips a duffel, taking out an enormous electric airchisel, red and shining in the dim light from the alley.

'Will you look at this thing?' Sean whispers, running his hand along the shining metal. 'Top of the line. You've got to be in the construction guild to get one of these. Nils must have paid someone a lot of cash for it.'

'He'll get it all back, you can be sure of that.' I look at the dull silver handle of the airchisel, worn by honest labour, not nightwork like ours. But the machine stayed the same, unaligned.

Gerry rushes back in, a dirty red cable trailing behind him. 'We're ready. Connect.' Sean finds the plug and pushes it into the cable. He reaches down and lifts the airchisel up on its point, putting one foot up on a footrest. He presses the button on the handle and the airchisel roars to life, bouncing up and down until Sean loses his grip and it falls over on the floor with a crash.

'Run one of these before?' Gerry shoves Sean out of the way and lifts up the chisel, checking it for damage.

'Yes. Maybe,' he says.

'It doesn't take any brains. That's why we brought you along.'

'I didn't mean to start it up.'

'Then don't press the trigger, slowboat.'

Sean's eyes twitch. 'Okay, okay.'

Gerry pushes a desk toward the wall and clears off all the faded photographs of long-dead children away with the back of his hand. 'You still watching the door, Ian?'

I nod and lean out into the hallway. I can see the back door and the alley through the narrow window bars. It is light now, almost morning. At the end of the alley, people drift through the square in ones and twos. Above them, low clouds keep the light dim, the battered sidewalks unmarked by shadows. A yellow day, safe enough. A day when people leave the city or stay in their settles. A good day to steal, though it doesn't feel like one so far.

'I can only drill for a little bit at a time,' Gerry explains. 'Otherwise, someone may hear us and wonder what's going on. So cut us off after a count of twenty or so.'

Gerry stands on the desk holding the point of the airchisel against the wall while Sean leans into the handle. 'Now,' Gerry says. Sean presses the button.

A fierce roaring fills the office, so loud that my hands fly up to my ears. Bits of plaster flow, then grey cement. Gerry presses his eyes shut against the chips. I watch the end disappear into the wall, then remember what I am supposed to be doing and count to twenty.

'Stop,' I say, but they can't hear me. I run over and tap

Sean's shoulder. He takes his finger off the button.

'Wait about ten seconds until everything's quieted down.' Gerry looks at the small hole in the plaster and shakes his head. 'This could take a while.'

Once there were alarms, sensors, software to protect the cash hoarded in Depositor's Trust. Now there are just thick walls, and patrols with stoppers.

Gerry pulls the airchisel out of the wall and moves it up a few inches. He leans against the handle and Sean presses the trigger. Again, roaring fills the room. A larger chunk of plaster falls off the wall and bounces to the floor. Dust rises up and I taste it, sour and dry as rye flour. After twenty seconds, I tap Sean's arm again and we wait silently for a few moments, the airchisel's roar echoing in our ears. Gerry nods toward the door and I check it again. No one.

I tap Sean's arm and he starts to drill again, higher this time.

After almost an hour, Gerry and Sean have drawn a square of holes up the side of the wall. Chunks of plaster are thick on the floor and the raw grey cement sparkles in the dim light. I can see rocks in the cement and steel reinforcing rods thicker than my thumb. Each rod takes three or four turns with the chisel to break in two, sparks flying. It seems impossible that we will ever get to the other side.

We stand staring at the wall during brief breaks, as if we can break through it with our hard gazes.

'I'll be the lookout for a while,' Sean says, wiping the sweat from his nose with the back of his sleeve.

Gerry shakes his head. 'You stay on the hammer, Sean. That's what you're good for.'

We stare at the impenetrable wall. Gerry pulls at one of the reinforcing rods. 'They really used to know how to build,' he says. 'Hadn't counted on these. That's the truth.'

Sean rolls his eyes.

Gerry squints and puts his palm against the wall, as if trying to heal it. He shakes his head slowly. 'Of course, everything I say is a lie. Even when I tell you I'm a liar. Heard that one? The Liar's Paradox.'

'Pair of what?' Sean squints.

Gerry turns to me. 'Your father liked to talk about it, Ian. Had all kinds of ideas about it. He was brilliant. Never really sure how he ended up as a printer.'

I think about my long-dead father, wish he were here with us.

'Let's get back to it. We've got a lot of work ahead of us.'

Sean and Gerry lift the chisel and place it against the wall. The excitement has worn off, and they move slowly and carefully, wasting no energy. We will be here all weekend and it makes no sense to get tired this early. Sean presses the trigger and the chisel roars again, spraying up a fountain of cement fragments. When their eyes are pressed closed against the sour dust, I am the only one in the room watching. I stalk around the room, look down the hallway at the alley door, pick up pieces of stone that have rolled outside the doorway. All the while, time ticks away, an eternity in twenty short seconds. I count them like paper clicking through a press – fifteen, sixteen, seventeen, eighteen …

○ ● ○

The pressroom was my school long before it was my job. While the presses clanged away in the background, I drew on scrap paper and read in the corner near the ink table. During long runs, my father knelt by me and taught me. One day he took a piece of slate and wrote the letter *A* on it in chalk. He held it up to me.

'What is this?' he asked.

'A letter,' I said, then went back to reading. I was seven, and learned the alphabet years ago, could read better than my friends. I was already proofreading simple jobs for some of the printers for a little extra cash.

'It's not just a letter. It stands for something.'

'A is for Alliance,' I said, quoting the prop from school.

He shook his head. 'It stands for more than that.'

A pause. No other answer came to mind. I didn't understand what my father wanted from me.

He held the slate up. 'This is knowledge,' he said simply.

I nodded.

'It starts with one letter and leads on from there.' My father thrust the slate at me. 'Taste it,' he demanded, holding the slate close to my mouth. His dark-eyed gaze held an intensity that told me this was no ordinary lesson.

I stalled for a moment, then stuck my tongue out tentatively and ran it along the slate, picking up white chalkdust on its end and leaving a dark line.

'How does it taste?' he asked.

'Bitter.'

'Yes,' he said triumphantly, his point proven. 'Others will tell you that knowledge is sweet. You'll get plenty of sweet knowledge at the academy soon enough. But remember, always remember, that some knowledge is bitter.'

I nodded.

'Say it.'

'Knowledge is bitter,' I said.

'Saying the words is one thing,' he said. 'Learning it is quite another – a lesson only time will teach you.' With those words, our lesson drew to a close. My father went back to the press and I started reading again, the chalkdust lingering in my mouth like an ancient potion, one meant to cure innocence.

By noon the air is so thick with dust that we can hardly see across the room. Gerry is whitened by it. When he stands still he looks like a statue of himself, a fat printer in repose.

Only the trails of sweat that course down his face mark him as human. He squints at the hole and shakes his head. 'We got miles to go,' he says. 'Let's switch.'

'I can do it,' Sean says.

'I know that. But I can put more weight into it.' He waves Sean toward the front of the drill but he stays, shaking his head.

'Just move it, Sean. It doesn't matter.' Gerry pushes him toward the wall.

Sean spins around. 'Don't touch me.'

Gerry points his thick finger at Sean's chest. 'You're working for me. Let's get that straight.'

Sean shakes his head. 'We're all working for Nils.'

'And Nils put me in charge.' Gerry's jaw clenches and the muscle twitches as his daemonmill starts to turn.

'Just do what he says, Sean,' I whisper.

Sean pauses for a moment, then walks to the front of the chisel and jerks it from the floor.

'Honestly. Send an apprentice to do a man's work, and look what happens,' Gerry says, unsmiling.

Sean turns and shoots him a wither. 'Elder,' he mutters. 'Air-waster.'

'Old and wise enough to know a few things. What the hell do you know how to do, Sean, besides how to drink ... and sweep up around the presses?'

Before Sean can answer, Gerry starts up the airchisel and leans into it. Bigger pieces of cement fall to the floor now, and by the time I stop Gerry he has hammered off a whole section, which drops with a heavy thud.

'See. That's what happens when you're working hard instead of hardly working.' Back in the pressroom, Gerry rode all his assistants hard, until they quit, or crossed over to work for Sevenheads.

Even with Gerry behind the chisel, the wall still seems impossibly thick. We stop for a few minutes, grey dust covering everything in the office, flare sputtering in the corner. Sean and I sit on one side of the room, Gerry on the other. He takes a square of synth cheese from his pocket, cuts it up with his knife and tosses a piece to me, then to Sean, who lets his fall on the floor among the rubble.

'Don't complain if you get hungry later.'

Sean just stares at the floor. I've never seen him so seethy before. I nudge him with my elbow but he moves away.

'In a serious mood today,' Gerry says, chewing. '*Pensive,* even. A black day of the soul for our slowboat.'

'Don't call me that.'

Gerry pushes his unshaven chin at Sean, narrows his dark, shining eyes. 'Slowboat.'

Sean shakes his head. 'I said don't call me that.'

Gerry tightens his fists. 'Slowboat.'

'I said don't.'

'Slowboat. Slowboat. Slowboat.'

Sean walks over to the airchisel and bends down, struggling to pick it up by himself. He puts the point against the wall and presses the trigger, starting the roaring again, loud as the pressroom running at top speed.

Gerry just watches, shaking his head. In a few moments, Sean pulls the hammer out of the wall. It falls on the desk, then slips out of his hands and rolls onto the floor.

Gerry jumps up and shoves Sean aside, bends down to check on the airchisel. 'You break this and everything is off, Sean – everything. So if you can't be smart, be careful. This piece of equipment is irreplaceable … and worth a lot more than you are.'

Sean wanders around the room, kicking at the chunks of cement, reminding me of the way he used to act back at the academy when he had to learn something he didn't want to.

Gerry picks up the chisel and sets it heavily on the desk, then waves me over. 'Sean's causing problems,' Gerry whispers in my ear. 'Any idea what's up with him?'

'Just nervous,' I say.

'Okay. But is he going to snap out of it? Because I can't have him mess this up. There's lots of cash in it for all of us. I can go back to the guildhall and get an apprentice who knows how to work.'

'I heard that,' Sean says from across the room.

'Then wake up!' Gerry shouts. 'We got a lot of work to do, and we don't have a lot of time. So are you going to start putting out a little more, or do I have to go talk to Nils?'

Sean looks Gerry in the eye. 'Go talk to Nils.'

'You serious?'

Sean nods.

'You know what'll happen then, don't you? He'll write this job off as a mistake, a failure. And I don't feel like becoming part of that litany just because of you.'

I sit on a desk and watch Gerry circle the room. Sean pauses for a long time, considering the concrete rubble on the ground as if each piece were an ancient riddle. 'I'll keep going,' he says finally. 'But under one condition.'

'What's that?'

'You treat me with respect.'

Gerry laughs. 'What am I, your *father*? All I need you to do is hold the end of the chisel up against the wall, Sean, so we can drill some holes in it. Respect or no respect, we have to get through. But if giving you respect is going to make the drilling go faster, you got it. I respect you. The whole guild respects you. Our entire sector bows down to you, the prince of the West End.'

Sean frowns. 'Now you're making fun of me.'

'No, I'm just trying to lighten the mood. It's like the Chaos in here, everyone gone all dark. Meanwhile, the clock is ticking. The clock is definitely ticking.'

'Let's go,' Sean mutters. He lifts the end of the chisel and jams it in the wall. Gerry picks up the heavy handle and presses the button. The roaring starts again.

While they drill, I step back into the hallway to make sure

our noise doesn't attract any attention. I freeze. An Alliance smug stands in the centre of the alley, his grey uniform crisp, Special Privileges pin sparkling in his ear. I blink, wondering if the smug is simply a stock enemy summoned up by my fears. Or is it Keith, trailing my path through the city? The smug is shorter and thinner than my classmate, though just as real. He stares down at a pile of rags at his feet.

I back up slowly into the room, tap hard on Gerry's arm. 'Turn it off,' I shout.

The drill stops. Gerry starts to say something but I cut him short. 'There's a smug in the alley.'

Gerry picked up a bullybar from the floor. 'Let's take a look.'

Sean says nothing, just closes his eyes and raises his face toward the ceiling. He shakes his head, sure that this is the end of us all.

I lean down to knock out the flare. We creep slowly to the front of the office, careful not to bump against any debris. We peer out through the barred window. The smug stands in the alley, bored. He is young, probably no older than Sean and I. His black hair is slicked back, uniform carefully buttoned, tall black boots shining. He didn't grow up crawling through tunnels under the city. But if I were born a couple of sectors away, perhaps I'd be wearing a grey uniform now instead of dust-covered drabs. The Alliance is just another guild, one that manufactures power – political, economic, electrical – and carefully controls its allocation across the city.

The bundle of rags at his feet moves a little, revealing a man sunken inside a dirt-coloured coat, his leathery face dusted with white stubble. I recognize him as one of the wanderers of our sector.

'What's going on?' Gerry asks.

'The smug's talking to a scrambler,' I say. 'I used to see him around the guildhall, but he hasn't been around lately.' Looking down from the pressroom, I used to see him in the alley, locked in vigorous debate with the air. 'Guess he drifted over to Shattuck. Food's better here.'

The wanderer says something that he thinks is funny, laughing so hard that his face turns red. He bends in on himself, opaque eyes wet and sparkling.

Whatever he is saying is lost to us, too far away to hear. But the smug doesn't find it amusing. He looks up and down the alley for a moment, then lifts a polished black club high over his head and brings it down over and over again, as if hammering a post into the ground. The wanderer's mouth opens and I can hear his howling. Then the smug's face turns red and spit flies from his mouth. He brings the club down one last time. Then he takes his gleaming stopper from his holster and points it toward the wanderer's heaving body.

I duck back in the room.

Gerry grabs my shoulder. 'What's going on?'

'He's got his stopper out.'

Sean lurches forward but Gerry stops him. 'I don't think you should do that, slowboat. Let nature run its course.'

I crouch back though the hallway again and look out. The smug holds his stopper a few inches from the wanderer's ragged coat. He presses the trigger and sends out the stopping pulse. For a moment, a wavering blue beam connects the weapon and its latest victim. I can almost imagine that the smug is relighting the guttered flame of the wanderer's soul. But even from here, the pulse sends out a painful radiant pressure, as if we are at the bottom of a deep ocean. Then it stops, and we surface again. The wanderer lies still, eyes staring at the low grey sky. The smug puts his stopper away and looks around quickly, checking that no one saw him. He swaggers down the alley, as if culling has given him new vigour.

Gerry creeps forward and stands by me. 'Tell me what's happening.'

'The smug's leaving.'

'For now. But what if he comes back? Of all the places for

this to happen, it has to be right where we're trying to get some work done.' Gerry turns and kicks the dentist chair.

'What about the air-waster?' Sean asks.

'Culled.' Once people killed each other with ancient weapons – bullets, mortars, bombs, and missiles did their killing from a distance. But culling is personal and tangible. The stopper has to be held a few inches from the heart to work. Still, each new culling anneals us to the next.

'Remember this, young friends. Just because someone's wearing a uniform instead of drabs doesn't mean he's not crooked. Smugs around here don't care about anything except getting cash from Sevenheads. He has this whole sector bought off.'

'Just like Nils back in the West End,' Sean says.

'Except Nils would never let anything like that happen,' Gerry says with vehemence. 'You don't know all the good things he's done. Getting us through the Chaos. Keeping us in cash and oxygen.' He turns from Sean to me. 'Paying your father's salary years after he …'

'After he what?'

'After he was culled in an accident,' Gerry says flatly. 'Out on a job for Nils.' He walks back to the drilling room.

'Liar,' I whisper. My father's path from printer to martyr was clouded by a litany of uncertainties. Why did he go out when the sensors said stay? Why hadn't he gone into a shelter? Why had he fallen within sight of the guildhall, sprawled on the dusty streets of the West End?

We go back to the wall, the chisel barely scratching the cement. We think only of getting inside, already forgetting the nameless scrambler lying dead in the alley, his wandering days through.

Late in the afternoon, Sean pushes the airchisel through the wall. Gerry gives a weary smile and puts his heavy hand on my narrow shoulder. An hour later, the hole is big enough for us to crawl through. We are in. We push the duffelbags through, then stand for a moment, waiting for some hidden signal to send us ahead.

'Go!' Gerry shouts, neck corded.

I go first, then Sean, and finally Gerry struggles through the narrow opening, cursing Sean for not cutting its edges more carefully. Dust-covered and heaving, we stand in the quiet bank lobby for a moment.

'Guards are supposed to come by and look around, but they never do, particularly on a holiday,' Gerry says.

'How do you know?' Sean asks.

'Nils checked it out.'

'What if they find Mr. Sullivan and figure it out?'

'That's just something we'll have to deal with when it comes,' Gerry says. 'Uncertainty is part of any job. Makes it exciting – right, Ian?'

I look at Gerry, say nothing.

'I mean, a story isn't exciting if we already know where it's going, what the ending is.'

Again, I have no answer. All I want is for the ending to be here already, for us to be crawling out of the bank rather than into it.

Ahead of us waits the lobby, a low cement wall and chain-link fence that separate the bankers from the customers, with a small hand-through cut in the metal to let the cash flow in and out. During the Consumption, cash travelled by wire across sectors and frontiers, pooling in electronic oceans. But the Chaos ended all that, returned us to ancient ways.

We walk to the back, past the enormous vault, battered blue steel with levers and dials circled with chipped numbers. 'Behind this door, there's enough cash to keep the guild going for years,' Gerry whispers. 'But we have to leave it alone.'

Sean stops. 'Why?'

'Guards can see it from the entrance. Sometimes the door

is rigged to explode. Or they lock vicious dogs inside. It's too dangerous.'

'Being dangerous never stopped you before.'

Gerry turns to Sean as if explaining something very obvious. 'The people who keep their money in the vault are honest drabs who trust the bank. It's not where Sevenheads keeps his cash.'

We walk on along the tile floor, darkened by the steps of bankers and their clerks who walk from office to office, venture toward the fence to parcel out cash. Deeper in the bank, the offices are wood-panelled, with oil paintings on the walls and marble statues balancing on pedestals in the dim corners.

'Old style.' Gerry shakes his head. 'They ought to charge admission.'

We pass a door with gold letters marking it as the office of James Sullivan, vice president.

We stare at the name for a moment and I remember the silver nailhead shining in his elegant, greying hair. Then Gerry pulls back and spits on the window. We move on, stopping at a heavy metal door. Gerry points and Sean opens it quickly with his bullybar.

Peering in, we can see a long thin room, L-shaped and lined with safe deposit boxes. We slip inside quickly, and Gerry shuts the door behind us. Sean sparks a flare. Clerks shuffling to retrieve boxes year after year have worn a trail along the tile floor. Gerry and Sean look at the boxes, lined up like squares in an enormous grid of numbers that stretches far into the distance. I close my eyes and shake my head at the enormous scale of our outside job for Nils.

'One of these boxes holds Sevenheads' cash, millions of it,' Gerry says, setting forth our challenge for the weekend. 'We find it, we win. We'll be lush. And their guild will be in real trouble. Nils keeps some cash here too, so we'll have to knock open our box as well. And we'll open up as many others as we can.'

'Why?' Sean runs his fingers along the rows of boxes, turns a numbered dial and pulls on it. It stays shut.

'So the Alliance doesn't think it's us,' Gerry says. 'They'll think it's the opposition or some ordinary scav.'

Gerry drops the duffelbags on the floor and reaches inside one to pull out a long steel bar with a narrow tip. It's an ink roller from one of our largest presses.

'It got bent,' Gerry says. 'No good for printing any more, but the right tool for this job.' He puts the narrow end against one of the locks and pulls back, then thrusts it forward, leaving a dent in the box. A second thrust pushes the lock in and the door pops open. Gerry puts down the roller and pulls out the metal box behind the door and sets it gently on the floor.

We kneel over the box to watch as Gerry opens the top, slowly. He paws among a stack of papers and finds a few gold coins, a tangle of necklaces, a stack of browning photos, and a small metal box. He opens the box and a tiny golden cloud floats down on the papers.

'What the hell was that?' Sean asks.

'Hair. Baby hair, probably.' Gerry tosses the box on the floor, shaking his head. 'People will save anything if they have a place to keep it. Sentimental-like.'

We stand for a moment, staring at a stranger's collection of prized possessions, mostly worthless.

Gerry turns to us. 'Here's how it's going to go. We have to crack the boxes as fast as we can. Sean, you'll hold the end and aim it at the lock. I'll push the bar. We'll switch off.'

Sean nods.

'Ian, you pull out the box and scav through it. Put any cash, gold, or anything else that looks valuable and small in one duffel, pile all the other stuff in another for later. Wouldn't want to miss anything. We'll start with the larger boxes – Sevenheads is more likely to need one to hold all his cash.'

We nod, and without waiting to go through any more

details of his plan, Gerry sets it in motion, raising the steel bar and smashing it into the next box. Sean reaches up to steady the bar with one hand and guide it toward the lock, which pops in after a few hits. I pull the box out and kneel on the floor while Sean and Gerry move on.

I stare at the closed box for a moment with the anticipation of an archaeologist opening a tomb. Then I open it. On top is a stack of letters written in a spidery hand. When I push them aside, I find a ceramic cat, a well-thumbed ledger and a ring of rusted keys. It's more debris, with nothing of value to us. I carry the box down to the end of the narrow room and dump its contents unceremoniously in the corner. Then I push the box back into its slot just in time to pull out the next one.

Again I kneel in anticipation. What waits in the box? Cash for the guild? Sevenheads' motherlode? Or just some nameless drab's memories? I open the box and find three thick stacks of cash held together with string. I hold them up.

'Now we're getting somewhere,' Gerry says, pushing the metal shaft toward the next lock. His face is already red and sweaty from pushing the heavy bar. 'It's like I always say – *Give a man a fish and he'll eat for a day. Teach a man to steal fish, and he'll eat for a lifetime.*' He laughs; there are no fish.

I throw the cash into one empty duffel, some of the unsorted debris into another.

We move as a team, our differences reconciled in the simple work of freeing the boxes and gleaning them. Like all guilds, we have a secret plan – to accumulate all the cash we need to survive. Behind it waits my own plan, to gather the cash I need to take Melina far from the city. When I was younger, I wanted nothing more than to print and steal, to live by my fine eye and sharp wits as my father did. A foot soldier for Nils. Now I want more. Or, in truth, less.

As we work, my thoughts stray to Melina in Mrs. Boyle's settle, waiting for me to take her to *terra voluptatis*, our provo heaven.

○ ● ○

Just a week earlier, Melina and I walked the harbourfloor hand in hand on a green day. We passed through the forest of rocks and rotted pilings at the old wharves and wound down the gradual hill of the inner harbour, once crowded with tankers and container ships. Now the retreating tides left it dry and empty save for the wandering bands of scavs and lovers rolling in its hidden caves.

We took the sandy path straight toward the oceanside, still beautiful even in the aftermath of all that transpired here. To both sides, the rocks of the old coast were thick with the blue shells of mussels shattered by crows and decades of walkers. Moving lower, we walked on packed sand and salt, the crust broken by dozens of footpaths and holes where scavs had pried rusted metal from the ground.

Melina's limping smoothed here; it was one of her favourite places. Away from the crowded rooms of the opposition, she seemed happier, her mind clearer. She stopped every few moments to pick up a shell or piece of waterworn glass that appealed to her. She showed each to me as if it were a rare jewel, then put it into her pack.

Her thoughts were like a tumbled cabinet, still retaining order amid the intertwined debris. If I left her alone here on the path, she wouldn't know how to get back to Mrs. Boyle's settle. She would drift off to join the lost and abandoned who wandered the city.

The hill flattened and the harbourfloor turned mud-crusted, dotted with hidden artefacts that left low mounds along the path. Melina pulled a short length of rusted pipe from the ground and carried it with her. We came to a promising bump on the ground and she scraped the crusted mud to uncover an ancient bottle, its top sealed with a rusted metal cap. The bottle was narrow and painted with white and red swirls. Inside splashed a dark, opaque fluid – some brand of medicine.

'Beautiful,' she said, her first word in hours.

I took the bottle in my hand. Years underground had reduced the italic words painted on the bottle to unreadable ciphers. I read that it contained a litre, that it was returnable.

'Good one?'

'Not really.' Collectors in the city paid more for obscure Retail artefacts. I identified this one as a commonplace, a major brand, hardly worth carrying home. Melina started to put the bottle in her pack but changed her mind and set it upright along the trail, a totem of the Consumption for a scav to take back to the city and sell. We walked on.

'This reminds me of looking through my father's things,' I said.

'Did he keep them outside on the ground?'

'No, in his desk. I used to go through it while he was up working in the pressroom.'

'Mrs. Boyle screams when someone bothers her desk.'

I nodded.

'What did you find there?'

'Keys. Lighters. Old coins. Guild pins. A type magnifier.' Each hinted at an entire, mysterious world. The stack of letters from a woman in another sector suggested even more.

'Why did you look at them?'

'Because they were interesting. And every son wants to know his father's secrets.'

Melina turned and stared at me. 'I like the way you look at me,' she said. 'Everyone else does this.' She looked at the ground as she walked, eyes averted. People in the city didn't want to see limping, cloudy eyes, damage.

We walked on. In a few minutes, Melina pushed the rusted pipe into raised ground to unearth a yellow plastic box no bigger than her hand. She handed it to me. 'What is it?'

I looked at the pitted yellow plastic, ran my fingertip along the thin line marking the frequencies and volumes, the rusted metal inputs and outputs. 'A radio. They listened to them when they walked. Even when they ran.'

'Why?'

'Warnings, I guess,' I shrugged. 'Which sectors to avoid. When the attacks were coming.'

I handed it back to Melina and she held it to her ear, like a child might hold a large shell and expect to hear the ocean or ancient broadcasts echoing. But she heard nothing. She set the artefact by the dusty path.

During the Consumption, factories churned out these works of perfect beauty, so many that no one even bothered to notice how beautiful they were. People simply bought them, used them, and threw them into the ocean when they were done. Had I lived in that time, I'm sure I would have done the same. Now we gathered this lost time's leavings in collections and museums, kept our secret longing for Retail and its infinite choices hidden like a harbourfloor relic.

Each era has its discontents and desires.

The Consumption's complaints were lost now, unrecorded in any book I had read. In that time, there were unlimited choices – alt versions of the same products, different sectors to live in, various jobs. I was born in the Chaos, after the choices evaporated like the ocean shallows.

Ahead lay the enormous tanker, split open along its side. I could see inside the ship's honeycombed hull, partitioned now into provo rooms. Far above, couples lay intertwined on kapok mattresses, women cooked over smoking coals, children bounced a ball on the metal walls – hundreds of settlers in all, each separated by the steel dividers, unconcerned that any walker could see them. Torches sparked in the ruined bow of the tanker, where scavs gradually cut away the steel and let it fall soundlessly into the salted dust far below. They had been cutting for all the years I had been coming to the harbourfloor and the ship never seemed to get any smaller. We walked on.

Ahead, we saw the blue-black crows walking along the damp ground. They pulled at seaworms and crabs, fought with each other for findings.

'What are you looking at?'

'A message.' The crows scuttling feet scratched runes in the crusted sand.

'What does it say?'

'Nothing. Just letters.'

'Letters in a row make words, words in a row make sentences,' Melina said in a sing-song voice, reciting something she had typed for Mrs. Boyle. 'Sentences in a row make a manifesto. A manifesto can change the world.'

'I don't think the crows are writing a manifesto.'

'Maybe they are, but you just can't read it.'

I nodded, knew enough not to dismiss the possibility.

The sand turned darker as we came closer to the retreated ocean. I stopped and pointed at the ground. 'I can make water appear from the ground.'

Melina shook her head.

'Close your eyes.'

Dutifully, Melina closed her eyes. I cupped my hands and shovelled the sand, digging a hole about a foot deep, smelling of rot, salt, and chemicals.

'Open your eyes.' I said. 'Now watch.'

Grey seawater seeped into the bottom of the hole. In a minute, the hole was nearly filled.

Melina's eyes widened. 'How did you do that?'

'Magic,' I said, though I knew better. There was no magic any more.

I dig deep into the bank's version of the crusted harbourfloor. The debris is cleaner here, but no less common, the valuables mixed in with worthless paper. I pull out the next metal box and run my hand under the stacks of yellowed folders, finding nothing.

Printer's Devil

A few boxes later, I pull out a silver candlestick and a small set of silver cups. I hold them high.

'Not bad,' Gerry says. 'Put them in with the cash.'

Plundering the boxes is like reaching deep into a stranger's memory and sorting it for any chance bit of wisdom. I find photos of dogs, children's toys, a dozen thimbles, bracelets and wedding rings, silverware, books, a bottle of unrecognizable grey fluid, and all manner of disks and tapes encoded with information, images, all beyond retrieving now. Freed from their boxes, all objects that I find fall along a continuum of value. It sickens me to see existence reduced to debris, or maybe the air is growing thinner.

We pound on beneath the dull yellow glow of sulphur lamps, box after box opening at the end of Gerry's steel. Some take only one hit with the bar to open, others are harder. Individual as oysters, the boxes yield up an occasional pearl, and the layer of cash lining the duffel thickens with each passing hour. It might not be the motherlode, but it's adding up.

The next box holds a set of locked diaries. I dump them into the duffelbag of debris – there might be cash hidden between the pages. Then on impulse, I pick up one of the leather books and break its clasp with a hard pull. Choosing a page at random, I read – *Tues: a drink with Thomas, he has no idea.* A photo falls out – an ordinary man in a grey cap and tiny glasses. Is he the deceived or the deceiver? I let it fall. The floor of the vault room is littered with letters and diaries among the hair and teeth and photographs and expired Alliance docs. The vault room disgusts me with its persistent, tainting smell of memory, desire, and regret, which clings to my hands long after I have scattered the evidence on the floor.

Gerry sleeps, his head tilted back to reveal the lively welts along his neck. Sean curls in the papers. Exhausted, I stare at the continental stains on the ceiling. I think of walking across a field of green grass with Melina, staring up at a blue sky and charting the slow progress of white, pure clouds. There is no black wind or coryalis, no wind at all except for a gentle breeze pushing through the trees to reveal the silver undersides of leaves. This could be *terra voluptatis,* the pleasure lands I imagine waiting somewhere north of the city. Or perhaps I am becoming a sunriser like the rest, imagining that wishes alone might make the world whole again, like dreams of Retail.

    I rise and step quietly out of the vault room and into the bank lobby. From the front window, I look out on Shattuck Square and the enormous glimmering S, lit by fires at its base. Smoke trails up from its hidden dwellers. The streets are dark except for emergency lights that flicker with the grid. I watch the rise and fall of the glowing lights and imagine that this ebbing glow charts the breathing of our city, forever failing and recovering. A sensor blinks yellow in the centre of the square. The air is changing. The air is always changing.

    Above the square, crows perch on a sagging banner that invites the city to a parade this holiday weekend. Beaks tucked under their wings, they rustle quietly, like children easing into sleep. Further above, the opalescent whorl of the coryalis gazes down on the square.

    I stand at the window, one of the bank's blank eyes. The heavy wooden front door is its mouth, always hungry for cash. Behind me, Gerry and Sean wait in the many-celled brain. Our outside job for Nils is more; it is a bank job of the mind. I laugh and decide I've been up for too many hours without full oxygenation.

    Across the square, two figures sit at an outdoor table, not moving, just watching the blinking sensor. They rise slowly – one large and the other very small – then walk away, unhurried though they are breaking curfew. I wonder what brings them here on a holiday weekend when anyone with any sense has left the city. But by then they are gone, creeping down through the alleys that lead deep into Shattuck, thick with wanderers, schemers, nightworkers of other guilds – all as intent on survival as we are.

During the Chaos, we heard hands beating against the steel walls of the guildhall at night, outsiders who wanted in.

Rival guilds came to the West End to challenge us. The ominous rhythm of their footsteps and their handslaps echoed through the building. The fishermen came on a hot summer night when the black wind was near and the Gnostics spread fear in all sectors. They cast their nets up on our pediments, then climbed up, wriggling in the net as their catch once did before the ocean retreated. We stood on top of the hall and poured black ink into their eyes to blind them, dropped pages of lead type off the edge to knock them from the walls. That failing, we melted the lead and poured a sizzling rain down on them. Blinded, damaged, the fishermen ran screaming back to the harbourfloor.

We had nothing against their guild, nor they against us. Fishermen know little of fonts, nor printers of fish. But they knew that our guild was thriving and that we had oxygen and cash. Theirs was failing; they were fishermen without fish. So they hated us and attacked us again and again. We repelled them each time, but with escalating violence and damage until, one day, the fishermen didn't come back.

Soon the musicians took their place, blaring their dented instruments to wake us and taunt us into battle. Ink and lead worked again, as did the forays of pressmen onto the streets, armed with press rollers that made scrap of their instruments and skulls.

Then came the bakers, failing from the flour shortage and rats.

It seemed that any guild could be our enemy if they were

desperate and jealous enough.

The guildhall was our ark, insular and rife with rumours and hidden signals. We were about to be attacked by the transport drivers. We were going to move to another sector. Down in the shelter, the mothers of our martyrs sent their wailing up over the thrumming presses. Nils sat in his office above us all, beyond reproach or rumour. He did what the guild needed, explained his decisions later or not at all.

As our suspicions grew finer in focus, the world turned partisan. Ink and paper were clearly on our side, but would the steel doors that protected us turn on us and let our enemies in? Would the gas we cooked with explode in our faces? Would water side with the fishermen and try to poison us? Would our ration of flour sympathize with the bakers and choke us?

Anything seemed horribly possible.

'Ian!'

Gerry's shouts take on a new urgency. I run to the vault room, slipping in to keep any light from flickering out into the lobby.

Gerry pikes boxes with his metal bar. 'Get slowboat to help.' He points at Sean, still curled up among the papers.

'Sean, hey. Wake up.'

'Not doing any more.' He turns away.

I lean down and whisper into his ear, smell his sour hair. 'Sean, the sooner we find Sevenheads' cash, the sooner we can leave.'

He sits up and rubs his eyes. A narrow line of smoke trails from the sulphur lamps and the air is thin and chemical. 'He's trying to choke us.' Sean points at Gerry.

'You're the one who's choking us, Sean, by not doing your part.' Gerry points back, eyes narrow and flashing. 'The longer we're here, the more likely the smugs will find us. It's not like we haven't been making noise, you know.'

Sean rises slowly and trudges through the debris.

'All you have to do is stand there, Sean, so I can steady the bar on your shoulder.' Gerry turns Sean toward the row of safe deposit boxes, some sprung open, others stubbornly locked. Gerry puts the heavy bar on Sean's shoulder, aims, then pushes the bar quickly toward a lock, knocking it in.

The force shoves Sean into the rows of boxes. He turns and pushes Gerry against the other wall. They slam each other around the room like schoolyard rivals.

'Stop it, both of you,' I shout, but they keep fighting. I turn to leave. 'I'm going back to the guildhall.'

'And I'm sure Nils will be very happy about that.' Gerry keeps Sean at bay with one thick, straightened arm.

'I don't think he'd be too happy about what's going on.'

'No, I don't think he would.' Gerry turns to Sean. 'All you got to do is just stand there, Sean. Simple as that.'

'Just don't shove me into the wall.'

'Brace your arms in front of you and it'll work, promise.'

'And I know what your promises are worth, you lying airwaster,' Sean sputters. 'I hope you choke.'

Our cell of three turns as toxic as the air around us. We are seethy and primed to hate. An alt version would have our brotherhood of thieves merrily plundering the boxes, glad to find cash. But that isn't true.

'I don't care what you think about me,' Gerry says. 'Say whatever you want. But we're all in this together. And until we find Sevenheads' cash, we've got to stay civil-like.'

Gerry rips back a door and hands the heavy metal box to me. Inside are glass paperweights, dozens of them. Some encase flowers and plants, others just coloured spirals.

Gerry picks one up and throws it at the end of the room, where it powders against the wall of boxes with a loud shatter.

I reach in the box and bring out a glimmering hammer, the

same size and shape as a metal hammer, but made of crystal, etched with complicated patterns and symbols, unrecognizable characters of an unfamiliar alphabet.

Gerry takes the shimmering hammer from my hand. 'Oh, this is rich,' he says, flipping the hammer and catching its delicate handle deftly in his thick fingers. 'A crystal hammer. What could be more superfluous, more Consumption?'

'Doesn't look that super to me.' Sean reaches up and tries to grab it, but Gerry pushes him away.

'Superfluous means useless. As in *you are superfluous to this job.*'

Sean stares at Gerry.

I take the hammer back and spin it slowly, watch the light refract blue and red from the shimmering handle. 'Why would anyone make a glass hammer?'

'Because they could,' Gerry shrugs. 'People could make anything back then, and look where that got us.' He grabs the hammer from my hand again.

'What do you do with a crystal hammer?' Sean asks.

'Plenty,' Gerry says. 'First, you save up your cash to buy it. Crystal was rare, you know, made from special sand, melted and carved by craftsmen. You could buy a cabinet to put it in, with lights that would show it off. Then you could sit in your house and stare at the crystal hammer while the rest of the world crawled in the dust and starved, the air heated, the carbon converged and the coryalis opened and…'

Gerry throws the hammer across the room. It spins handle over head then smashes against the far wall. 'That's better,' he says with satisfaction. 'A few thousand years from now, it'll be ground down to sand again.'

Sean reaches in the box, looking for more crystal to shatter. He digs deep beneath a layer of papers and pulls out a shining revolver made of steel, not crystal. His eyes brighten.

'Let me see that.' Gerry walks toward him but Sean backs away.

'Mine.' Sean opens the gun and spins its chambers, then puts it to his temple. 'Dare me?'

'From what I know, it looks like there's a bullet in every chamber, slowboat,' Gerry says. 'I'd have to say your chances aren't so good.'

'No, they're not.'

Sean seems like a stranger to me, a dust-striped stranger with a leering smile. 'Put it down, Sean,' I say carefully.

'Scrambler,' Gerry mutters.

Sean squeezes his finger slightly. Then one of the sulphur lamps burns out and the room dims. Sean looks at me suddenly.

'What're you staring at, Ian?' He lowers the gun.

'Nothing,' I say.

'That's right. Nothing and no one.' Sean tucks the gun into the waistband of his drabs. 'I'm keeping this, Gerry. In case you start going cold on us again, like you did on Mr. Sullivan.'

Gerry relights the lamp and the room brightens. 'Enough talk,' he says. 'We've got guild history to make.'

Sean shrugs, stands with his arms stretched out toward the wall, and lets Gerry put the heavy bar on his shoulder, aim, and push again and again to open a stubborn door.

Inside, the box holds two thick stacks of cash. I push the stacks into the duffel.

'That's more like it. Finally, a good sign,' Gerry says. A pause – there have been too many other signs already, none good.

'So far we've got about as much cash as we would if we had robbed a cornershop,' Sean says.

'We'll have a lot more when we find Sevenheads' box.' Gerry pushes the bar into a lock, pushing it in. 'It's here somewhere, I can feel it.'

'I don't get why we're always after Sevenheads,' Sean says, shrugging. 'How come we hate his guild? They're printers, too.'

'They're our enemies,' Gerry says. 'They want to take us over.'

'Don't we want to take them over, too?'

'Of course.'

'Then maybe we're the enemy.'

'They're not like us,' Gerry says. 'They print in a different way. We use ink. They use carbon pulled out of the air, the same stuff that chokes you. Remember, Sean? From back in school? *Then came the Convergence, when Two became Three?* It's about oxygen and carbon.'

'I remember,' Sean says, though I doubt it.

When Two Became Three. The ancients used the phrase to mean childbirth. But it came to mean something different during the Convergence – the dark passage of O_2 to deadly CO_2.

I reach up to pull out the next box, find only letters and ancient documents in filigree type – immigration papers, from the time when people could go where they wanted, not where they were told.

'I've seen them pull a truck up at a purification centre and take away tons of it,' Gerry says.

'The devil's dust,' Sean says.

'That's right, the devil's dust. They grind it down, spray it on paper and sell it as printing. They use electrostatic presses. Carbon flying everywhere. Their printers have to wear masks or they choke.'

'But they're still printers,' Sean says.

'They're a different kind of printer. And they hate us, not just because we don't use fonts with serifs. But because we have the Alliance on our side.'

'I still don't get it. We're all just printers.'

Gerry rolls his eyes, sure that Sean is being difficult. But Sean is right; there is no real reason behind it all.

'Like I said, they're different.' Gerry shoves his bar into a new lock, the metal sparking. 'They don't even have a guild-hall. They're scavs, setting up their shop wherever they want, moving on when they feel like it. Fully provo.'

'What did they ever do to us?'

'Plenty. We've got a litany of grievances a mile long. Ask Nils to show it to you sometime.'

'Like what?'

'They stole our land. Our guild used to control Shattuck, you know. Until they set up shop there.' Gerry shoves the bar again, pushing in the metal door. 'Sevenheads claimed some of our territory and started calling it his own. As if just saying it was his might make it true.'

'So what? There's plenty of printing to be done. We're already working all the time. Double shifts and all.'

'They threaten us just by existing. They'd do anything to have our presses, our guildhall, and our cash. Don't doubt it.'

'You're just saying that so we keep working,' Sean says.

'Believe me, Sevenheads wants to cull us all,' Gerry says. 'Given the chance, he would. In a minute. There's not enough air for everyone any more. Only the strongest get to keep breathing. Everyone else chokes. It's that simple. And given the option, I think everyone would rather keep breathing, am I right?'

I don't answer, just reach up and pull out the box, put it on the floor, and riffle through its contents with a practised sweep of my hand, freeing paper from cash, sentimental from valuable.

'Anyway, if it weren't for Sevenheads, Ian's father would still be alive instead of on the Martyrs' Wall.'

I stop, shoot Gerry a wither. 'What're you talking about?'

'I'm not saying any more. Nils told me not to. Said it would upset you – we all know how you are, sensitive-like.' Gerry lines up against another lock and pushes.

'What? Tell me.' I throw the metal box down on the ground, scattering paper across the floor.

'Not saying.' Gerry shakes his head.

I sit down. 'Then I'm not going through another box.'

Gerry leans on his pike. 'Fine, I'll tell you. But you have to promise never to tell Nils I said anything.'

I nod, ready myself for one of Gerry's lies.

'You were what, seven or eight when your father died?'

'Eight.'

'Back during the end of the Chaos, right?'

'Right.'

Gerry leans on his metal bar, hunches down toward his listeners. 'Back then, all printers had to do a sentry shift down at the main entrance to the hall,' he whispers. 'We'd work a press run, then go downstairs to make sure that no strangers got in, or that no one went out when the black wind was blowing. No one liked doing it much, but it was just a duty.'

We nod.

'The night your father was caught out in the black wind, Sevenheads was the sentry. Your father was delivering some docs across the city. Sevenheads knew the sensor was red, but he let him out. When your father came back later that night, Sevenheads left the door locked. He cast your father out. Your father choked right there in front of the guildhall while Sevenheads watched.'

'Why would he do that?'

'Not sure. Sevenheads claimed your father was trying to sneak back from seeing some woman in another sector and got caught in the black wind.' Gerry pauses. 'And maybe he was, who knows? But that's no reason to cast him out.'

I shake my head at Gerry's alt version, so different from the one my mother and Nils had told me. 'That's not the way I heard it. It was just an accident. He was just making a delivery for the guild. Just like anyone else, he got culled for being in the wrong place at the wrong time.'

'What's the difference between being cast out or just conveniently forgotten?' Gerry says. 'In any case, it wasn't an accident. Don't buy Nils' prop. He always makes every printer into a hero, a martyr for the wall. It's just not that clear.'

'But what was in it for Sevenheads?'

'This was back before Sevenheads betrayed us, you know. Your father was the best printer we had. I think Sevenheads was just trying to get rid of him. He was jealous.'

I say nothing, wonder how much of what Gerry told me is true.

'It's the truth, Ian,' he says, reading my thoughts.

'Nothing's true,' I say. 'It just depends on who you decide to trust.'

Gerry smiles for a moment. 'That's exactly the kind of thing your father used to say, intellectual-like.'

'Before Sevenheads cast him out,' I say.

'Right.' Gerry harpoons another box and I open it up, finding nothing but a box of childhood artefacts – a rattle, a pair of shoes, a stuffed rabbit. Maybe the black wind had culled the child as he played, or perhaps he had simply grown up. I don't care. I'm just doing my job, waiting for it all to be over.

We go back to work, moving in glum silence from one box to the next. I take no particular pleasure from the cash we find, except that each plundered box brings us that much closer to finding the fortune Sevenheads has locked away in the vault.

As we work, the air in the vault turns thinner, and my thoughts stray far from our littered tomb.

I picture a forest thick with crystal trees, clear and glowing, as if they have been forced out from the molten centre of the earth. A delicate lace of glass leaves hangs down to the ground. I shake my head to leave the glass forest behind. I don't have time to decipher imaginary worlds. It's hard enough to stay awake, to keep Gerry and Sean from culling each other, to find Sevenheads' carbon-tainted cash.

I pause for a moment over the latest battered box pulled from the wall, and will it to be lined with stack after stack of cash. Instead, I find only a faded wedding portrait, a dark-eyed bride and thick-waisted groom standing stiffly as if their hearts are stopped rather than full of love. Beneath the portrait, I pull docs from guilds that no longer exist, deeds to worthless property.

Anything that once held value seems to retain a glow forever. We walk on a thick layer of the once-valuable, shifting beneath our feet as we walk from box to box.

Gerry loses his footing and shouts at me to clear it all away. I shuffle my feet along the floor, herding the papers, photos, broken watches, deeds, infant slippers, and the rest all to the far end of the vault room. I shove as much as I can deep into one of the empty duffels, pressing it down with my boot so that I can push in more and more of it until the bag can hold no more. I close it and lock it away.

For a time we become guild brothers again. We work relentlessly for cash – as people did during the Consumption – heedless of any damage that we might be doing. The next box we open will hold Sevenheads' motherlode, setting us free of the vault room and its stink of sweat and dust. If not, then the next one. I burrow on, fuelled by hope, heedless of my mother's warning always to be careful what I hope for. After all, my father always hoped to be a printer, a desire that landed him on the Martyrs' Wall among hundreds of other printers. Swift, clever, dead.

Sean and I were fourteen when we threw our first provo bomb made from an ink jar filled with plate-cleaning solution and a twist of tightly wound cover stock as its fuse. Our band of apprentices broke curfew and travelled across the city to a storefront where Nils had heard a printer was setting up shop. PRINTER! New to the city, the innocent had emblazoned the word in red paint across the front of his store, proudly ignorant of the ways of the guilds. We shook our heads at his audacity. He might as well have painted FOOL! I cocked my arm back and Sean lit the fuse, then I sent the jar arcing across the street, fuse blazing like a comet's tail (or what I thought a comet's tail might look like). The low fire splashed across the broken sidewalk and flowed beneath the front door.

The building stayed dark for a moment and we took out a second jar, ready to touch flame to paper again. But then low orange fire glowed through the bars of the storefront windows. Burning a print shop was childswork, and we were the children to do it. The fool's paper and inks beckoned for the match. We ran back to our tunnel, turning to watch the progress of the flames, stretching higher now. PRINTER! would soon join the other burnt-out stores that lined the narrow streets of the city.

I would bring news of our victory to Nils, our father, leader, king of the West End, who would be proud of us. Our story would enter the guild's vulgate of heroic, violent acts. Printers one moment and soldiers the next. Sean and I had the cockiness of untested recruits, green and cruel, ready for any assignment, but underneath, afraid and ashamed of what we did.

We work slowly, three atoms orbiting in the finite universe of the narrow vault room. As I search through one box after the next, I watch Gerry stab at another lock, his blunt fingers white on the heavy pike. Sean leans against the wall of boxes, eyes half-open. I have hardly spoken to him in hours, unable to talk him out of his unshakable sullenness.

We are tired, low on air, deluded by fading hope. Once we

find Sevenheads' cash, we can leave the vault and Shattuck far behind. All will be right with the world. Defeated, Sevenheads will leave the city. We will thrive on his cash, as vital as blood or oxygen. If we don't find the cash, we will have to endure the quiet disappointment of Nils and clever remarks in the pressroom. How could we spend days just inches away from Sevenheads' cash and not be able to steal it?

I trudge to the back of the vault and cram the duffelbag with more photographs and papers, wills, and immigration docs. Another duffel is filling up with short stacks of cash, the occasional drawer of it. Do I feel a twinge of guilt at stealing from others? I suppose so, but I am too exhausted to consider much beyond the vault room's walls, its boxes half-sprung. I tell myself that we are just stealing from thieves, our guild's way. If anyone keeps money in a crooked bank, they are probably just as crooked, though I have no way of knowing that for certain.

Sean walks out of the vault without a word.

Gerry stares at him. 'Hey. Where do you think you're…'

'I'm sleeping for a few minutes,' he shouts. 'Can't stand it any more.'

I follow Sean out, watch as he kicks open Sullivan's office door and sprawls on the floor beneath a long wooden table stacked with the dead man's books.

'Leave me alone,' he mutters. 'Both of you. I just need to sleep.'

Before I can say anything, Sean is asleep on his back, eyes twitching beneath grey lids, low breathing echoing. I walk out of the office and stop for a moment at the bank's windows, see the dark sky over the square and the sensor blinking red. The front door opens easily from the inside. It would be easy to leave our failed mission and walk toward Mrs. Boyle's settle and Melina's warm cot.

Then Gerry shouts.

I rush back into the vault room and find his back pressed

against the wall. His metal harpoon points at the latest box, the door bent open, metal lid raised and waiting.

'What!'

'Look in the box,' he says softly. Sweat trails down his face and darkens his drabs at the neck and under his arms.

'What is it?'

His eyes burn with frantic intensity. 'Just look and tell me what you see.'

I take a few steps forward to look inside the box. I can make out a black shape, lit only by the vault room's flickering sulphur lamp. The blackness seems to absorb light, though a few patches sparkle. It's a doll blackened by fire. I have already unearthed an army of ancient dolls in the boxes, with smudged ceramic limbs and glass eyes that opened and closed as I pushed them aside, plastic babies limned with chemical moulds.

This doll is larger and made hideous by decay. As I step closer, I see that it doesn't have one face with blinking eyes, but seven heads, each as tiny and unformed as the next.

I run toward the door but Gerry reaches out and catches me with his heavy arm.

'What is it, Ian? Tell me.'

I shake my head, try to run away again.

Gerry blocks the way, puts his hands around my head, tilts my face up toward him. 'Tell me!' He stares at me, eyes wild and bloodshot.

'I think it's … it's Sevenheads' child.' I was in the guildhall that morning so many years ago, saw the bloodslick monstrosity in its bowl. Now it is desiccated and twisted by time, but still familiar.

Gerry lets go of me, shivers involuntarily for a moment, then recovers, turning back to the task at hand. 'Then that must be Sevenhead's box, the one where he keeps his cash. Make sense?'

I nod. Gerry tries to hand me his metal bar. 'Must be underneath it. Stacks of cash. Go take a look.'

'No.' I shake my head frantically.

'Then go get Sean. Let's make him do it.'

'I don't think that's a good idea.'

'Then we'll look at it together. Like brothers.'

Gerry was never a true brother to anyone in the guild. I have no choice but to follow him as he walks slowly toward the box, the tip of his harpoon leading the way.

'I'll lift it up,' he says. 'You look underneath.'

He pushes the sharp tip under the blackened carapace and lifts one side carefully, disturbing it from its reliquary. Tiny pieces of brittle skin shatter and fall into the box.

'Now look under, Ian.'

I inch forward and see only browning paper pocked with rot. 'Just paper.'

'Maybe the cash is underneath.'

'So?'

Gerry points. 'Reach in and check.'

'How?'

'With your hand.'

'No.' I shake my head. 'I'd rather choke.'

'Come on. Nothing to be scared of. It's dead. Definitely.'

'That doesn't mean I want to touch it.'

Gerry raises the body a little further, as if inviting me in. 'Go ahead.'

I inch forward because the evil gears of Gerry's mind are about to whirl into motion, fuelled by exhaustion and frustration. He could pike my skull as easily as any metal box.

I reach in to pluck out a piece of paper, then another. I can see the blackened skin's delicate coating of down, the seven identical heads, fourteen eyes pressed tightly closed, the bones pressing out against the skin like the ribs of a miniature ship. It's beautiful as an ancient body pulled from the grave, the gold scaved, only the desiccated flesh and steely sinews remaining.

My hand shakes as I push the paper away until I can see

the bottom of the box. 'Nothing.'

'Nothing?'

I turn to Gerry and shake my head.

He lets the blackened infant fall back into its box. 'After all that, no cash.' Gerry walks toward the box, eyes flashing.

I turn to face him. 'Don't.'

'Don't what, Ian?'

'Don't throw it across the room. Smash it against the wall. Whatever you're going to do.'

Gerry presses his red face next to mine and I can see the skein of pores and welts along his cheekbones, roasted from years of UVR. 'The air in here has scrambled you, friend. Made you strange.'

'Just don't throw it across the room.'

'Why not?'

'Because ... because I don't want to be walking on it.' But more: it would be bad luck. One desecration leads to another.

Gerry smiles. 'There's the spirit. Thought for a moment you'd gone soft.' He lifts the box and looks down. 'Ought to put this in some kind of museum. To warn people.'

'About what?'

'About what happens when you fuck with Mother Nature. How she fucks you right back.'

During the Chaos, mothers birthed hollow children, empty under their pale skin; bodies with limbs attached at obscene junctures; stillborn families of conjoined siblings. These horrors delivered the same message – it was no time to bring a child into the city.

Gerry carries the box out into the hallway. In a moment he's back, picking up his steel harpoon with new enthusiasm. 'We're not going to get lush on this job, but we may still find more cash. And I don't want to go back to Nils without a full bag.'

I nod. It's too late to stop Gerry. His eyes are narrow, dark pinpoints that skitter around the vault room. He won't quit until all of the boxes are opened. Sevenheads' cash – the whole reason for our job in the first place – eludes us. Still, Gerry wants to keep searching.

When I was a child, I respected Gerry, thought of him as an elder I could learn from. Now I know that anything he says is suspect. He is the Liar's Paradox in filthy drabs.

We work the boxes, saying little, just an occasional growl from Gerry as he shoves the harpoon and the rattle of my fast hands among the boxes. As if to reward us for our persistence, the boxes turn generous – not the motherlode we need, but stack after stack of cash until the duffel is almost full.

Hours tick by and I lose all track of their passing. I wander in and out of the vault room. Gerry frantically harpoons each tiny lock with his steel bar, unable to stop. Grey light filters down the hallway from the front of the bank and it is almost morning. Melina and Mrs. Boyle are waking in their settle, empty wine bottles lining the provo office. This week's issue of the *Sliver* will start with interminable arguing among the staff; the opposition is slow to rise and seldom agrees about anything.

I watch Gerry as he works, sweat running down his pale neck. Gerry isn't doing this for the guild; he is simply destroying and gathering the spoils.

A scream echoes through the bank, loud enough to be heard in another sector. We turn toward it, eyes narrow.

Sean runs in, face pale and streaked.

'It's here,' he shouts. 'I woke up and it was right next to me.'

'What?' Gerry says.

'The black ... the seven ...'

'That? We found it in one of the boxes.' Gerry leans against his steel harpoon, watches Sean stomping around the room. 'Sevenheads didn't leave any cash here, just a little petrified offspring.'

'And you put it next to me to scare me, didn't you, you worthless waste of air.' Sean's eyes turn wide and his fists clench.

'No, Sean, I just set it outside the door here, really.' Gerry glances at me and his horrible mouth turns up at the ends, twitching.

'You're a liar,' Sean shouts.

Gerry points at him. 'Yes, I put it next to you. It didn't walk there, did it? Thought it would scare you back to work.' Eyes blazing, fingers twitching, Gerry stalks toward Sean.

Sean reaches behind him, takes out the ancient gun he'd scaved, and points it at Gerry. Before I can tell him not to, Sean fires away and explosions fill the room, one after the next. Louder than the curfew blast. Louder than a high-speed press. Gerry falls to the ground, hands outstretched, as if he can stop the bullets. Shot after shot ricochets through the room, vectoring from one metal wall to the next, screaming past my ears.

The back of my hand burns suddenly and I fall facedown to the ground among the paper and debris, bent around my bleeding hand. I lie in the nest of paper wondering if we are all about to become martyrs. Gerry will fit right in among the rows of unsmiling printers who sacrificed themselves to keep Nils in power. But Sean is too young. His handsome dead face will bring on weeks of grieving from the women of the guild, wailing through the narrow streets of the West End. I don't want my mother to find my own pale face on the wall next to my father, both culled for the guild. And more: Melina needs me.

The vault room turns quiet and still. My ears ring from the explosions and my hand throbs from its wound, which leaves a raw red arrow that points across my wrist and down my index finger. I rise slowly from the thick layer of debris. Across the room, Gerry stands, rubbing his eyes as if he has been asleep. The air smells sharp and smoke gathers near the ceiling. Sean lies on his back, still clutching the pistol in his hand, its ancient bullets spent now. That the pistol worked seems remarkable; that the ricocheting metal hit no one even more so. I walk over to Sean, nested among papers.

'Sean!' I shout, but he doesn't get up.

Gerry walks closer, making a low groaning, an ancient animal voicing of fear and dread and anger. 'Slowboat!' he yells. 'Get back to work. I mean it.'

I reach for Sean's shoulder and pull him up, heavy and unmoving in my hands. Gerry reaches down and helps me raise him up. Sean's open eyes stare blankly at us, his lips move, but no sound comes. Then I see the ripped patch on his shirt and pull it back. Blood bubbles around a ragged hole in his side. I can hear the sucking sound of air moving in and out, the horrible gurgling in his throat. I press my hand against the wound to staunch it, to keep the air inside him, but instead blood gushes from his mouth, raining down on the papers, photos.

Sean's head lolls back and he goes limp.

'No!' I shout. 'No. No. No.' I hold Sean close, his blood staining my drabs. He stays motionless, indifferent to the world, and nothing I can do will change it.

'Culled,' Gerry whispers.

I lower Sean gently on the floor. 'It's your fault,' I shout at Gerry.

'He did it himself – you saw it, Ian,' Gerry says numbly. 'He started firing away and something must have caught him, a bullet, piece of metal…'

'You made it happen,' I say. 'You scared him with your stupid joke.'

'We're lucky we didn't get culled too.'

'Lucky?' I say. 'We're anything but lucky, Gerry.'

The room turns quiet for a moment. I bend over my own knees, rocking like a child.

Gerry puts his heavy hand on my shoulder. 'C'mon Ian, cut it out. We got to keep going.'

'Keep going?' I shout. 'I'm going, all right. I'm going to

go tell Nils about this.' I stand up, wait for Gerry to try to stop me.

Instead, he sits down slowly on the floor. 'Ask him what he wants us to do,' he says softly. 'Tell him we found Sevenheads' baby. But don't tell him I scared Sean with it. I didn't mean to.'

'What did you expect him to do?'

Gerry shrugs. 'I don't know. I'm tired, Ian. I'm sick, too, ask Nils.'

I say nothing, shoot Gerry a wither.

'I'm sorry, Ian. I really am.' These quiet words come from an alt version of Gerry I haven't seen before.

I stumble out of the vault room and through the quiet bank, as grey at midnight as it was grey in the evening light and every hour in between.

Fear culled Sean the way it had so many others. It made him lose his precision and do something foolish. I climb back through the broken wall and through the dentist's office, tears marking my passing. I am our guild's teller, but words fail me.

Sunday

Carbon 1196 ppm. Suspected inversion approaches from the seacoast, creating hazardous breathing and potential red conditions throughout all sectors. City residents are urged to stay on alert, entering shelters or oxygenated areas at midday if air quality deteriorates further. Unknown conditions prevail in evening. Methane lightning likely. Shelters open on an as-needed basis to authorized personnel only.

I walk down the centre of the street toward the West End, heedless of the curfew. Rats scatter in the gutters before me. Crows shift gently along the tops of the storefronts, watching me with obsidian eyes. Scramblers look out from dark alleys then turn, relieved to find I'm just another wanderer through the waking city.

In the darkness, I don't fear the black wind, though the sensors are all blinking red and I have to stop every few blocks to put my hands on my knees and breathe. The black wind might swoop down from the roiling grey-green sky and cull me. But there are other threats.

I stay aboveground all the way through Shattuck. If I am intended to meet up with Sevenheads or his men, so be it. I am scrambled, about to choke. When I close my eyes, I see Sean's pale face, blood pouring from his mouth. I see his familiar eyes, wide open and unblinking.

In the half-darkness, I stumble along the buckled sidewalks, through cratered remnants of parks, until I pass Division Street and cross into the West End. I know every break in the pavement, every empty lot of crackled dirt and bleached weeds, every settle and store, every scrawled message along the alleyways. *Air Is For All. Breathe or Leave.* I step over tunnel covers that lead into our secret passageways, to empty waystations and dank platforms.

I climb the familiar cement stairway to my mother's settle, thick with the smell of potatoes and bread. Her settle is on a lower floor; she is an elder and needs to be able to get to the guildhall quickly when the sirens sound. I let myself in quietly with my key and turn on the light in the kitchen. In the narrow mirror above the kitchen sink, I see that my shirt is dark with blood. I pull at the neck, the buttons clicking across the floor, and throw the shirt across the room. I wash my hand in the basin and the cold water on my skin helps calm my spiralling mind.

I am home now, but I still expect to find the walls honeycombed with boxes, a thick carpet of debris lining the floor. When I hear someone walking toward the kitchen, I think it might be Gerry, harpoon in his hand, shouting at me to keep working.

'You're back so late. It's almost morning.' My mother leans against the doorframe, backlit by the bedroom's flickering light. My father's old robe is wrapped double around her thin body and almost reaches the floor. Her worried eyes scan me for a moment, noting every detail.

'What's wrong, Ian?'

'Nothing, just tired.' Water drips from my face.

She picks up my shirt from the floor and squints at it. 'Are you hurt?'

'Not really. That's not my blood.' I dry my face, hands.

'Whose, then?'

'Sean's.'

'Did you two get in some kind of trouble?'

I think of lying for a moment but don't. 'Sean's dead.'

We have seen so much over the years that nothing surprises her – until now. She bends over as if a fist has hit her in the stomach. 'No, Ian. That can't be right.'

'It's not right, but it's true.' I pace through the kitchen, the drying water cool on my chest.

'What happened?'

I tell her everything about our job for Nils, starting with Mr. Sullivan, then taking her to the poisonous vault room. My mother is well-acquainted with the ways of the guild and its outside jobs. I add details when she asks for them, describe Sevenheads' child, Sean firing into the dead air of the vault room, the scream of ricocheting bullets. By the time the story brings us back to the West End, we sit at the kitchen table, stunned.

She shakes her head. 'Sean was so blessed, everyone's favourite.' She turns angry, eyes flashing, long, grey-streaked hair flailing. 'Your father would never have let this happen.'

'What could he have done?'

'He never would have put Gerry in that room with you. Everyone knows he can't be trusted. Your father said Gerry had a black heart. That he would do anything, absolutely anything.'

I nod, sure this is true. We sit quietly for a moment and I think of Sean crawling in the tunnels with me, Sean sleeping in the corner of the pressroom, Sean culled on the floor of the vault room. Outside the settle, the sky brightens by degrees to reveal the sepia streets of the West End. I hear people walking down the sidewalk and hate their living steps – so casual and taken for granted, one after the next.

'Don't let this turn you dark,' my mother says, looking up between her steepled fingers, the skin loose and waxen. I am surprised at how much older she looks than the mother I carry in my memory.

I shrug. Who can say what's dark any more? Once the unthinkable happens over and over, there is no room for optimism or gloom. We are neutral, *precision above all else*.

'Being around printers all your life hasn't given you a lot of hope,' she says. 'They're a cold guild, everyone knows it.'

'Could be worse ... I could be working for Sevenheads.'

'Sorenson was strange, but very intelligent. Your father liked him a great deal, admired his presswork. He just happens to be the enemy now.'

'But didn't Sevenheads cast my father out? Leave him to choke on the street? That's what Gerry told me.'

My mother shuts her eyes, shakes her head. 'Gerry's a liar, you know that. Save that question for Nils. At least he tells you the truth, or as much truth as he cares to tell you. Not that he ever told me much – I was just the martyr's wife. Why tell me what happened?'

Her eyes tear again and she wipes them on the back of her hand. 'Never believe their prop, Ian. Those men will say anything to get what they want. Just trust yourself – you're not like them. Not at all.'

My mother seems infected with a new-found honesty.

'Why didn't you tell me this before I joined the guild?'

'It wasn't important then. You had no choice. Now you need to know what you're leaving behind. We won't be sitting at this kitchen table again for quite some time, will we? You're leaving, yes?'

I pause. 'How did you know?'

She smiles. 'Because I'm your mother. That's what young men like you have to do. They leave their settles. Especially in this city.' She narrows her eyes at the grey window. 'Not a lot to keep you here any more.'

'Except you.'

'Except me, and I'm telling you to go.'

'You used to be such a...'

'A sunriser? Go ahead and say it.' She smiles, squeezes my forearm.

'An optimist,' I say. 'You know – *The coryalis is getting smaller every day. The Alliance will bring order back to the city* – all that.'

'All that prop?'

'Yes.'

'Given the alternative, I think it's better to err on the side of hope.' She looks toward the window, as if hope resided there in the low grey sky. 'If there's anything I've managed to teach you, that should be the one bit you carry with you, wherever you go. Being without hope turns you cold. Look at what it's done for your guild brothers with their dark hearts, scrambling for cash, doing whatever it takes to get it.'

I stand and take a new shirt from the pegs along the wall.

She reaches into a kitchen drawer and holds her closed hand out to me. 'Take this,' she says. 'Your father would want you to have it.'

She drops an ancient type magnifier into my hand, a round glass lens circled by brass and supported by three bent brass legs. I remember playing with it while he ran the press, handing it up to him when he needed it. I hold it to my eye and see the kitchen distorted and out of focus, then bring my fingers up to it and see the gritty maze of my fingertips.

I smile and put it in my pocket. '*Precision above all else.*'

'A lot of good that will do you, wherever you're going.'

'Melina and I are going to…'

She holds up her hand. 'Don't tell me. They'll be asking after you, you know. Nils. The Alliance. This way I can honestly say I don't know.'

She holds me close for a moment, eyes closed, her cool cheek pressed into my chest, then walks quickly back into the bedroom, closing the door behind her to keep out all the pain and worry about her wandering son.

I lie down on the bed in my room and sleep fitfully for a few minutes, without dreams. Then I take my backpack and leave my mother's settle, walking out on the street and into the failing air.

○ ● ○

The city stutters awake, the new morning full of portents. On the streetcorners, Gnostics proclaim that this is the day of redemption. Shopkeepers set up their wooden stalls, careful not to move too quickly and find themselves sprawled on the street. Elders cluster together, heads close as they share the morning's rumours. Above the West End, the coryalis watches the new day begin, reborn and free of history. The ongoing renewal of the world might have brought me consolation if I weren't so exhausted.

Deeper into the West End, the narrow streets give way to flattened lots of rubble and half-standing walls. Our guildhall rises from this bleakscape, standing alone like a brave cement soldier, far from other buildings that might make it vulnerable to fires and attack. Walking closer, I can hear the low throb of the presses, so insistent that my steps lock into the familiar rhythm. I pass inside through the security portal, waved in by an apprentice I barely know. To him, I am a hero, someone to be respected and emulated, a foot soldier doing an outside job for Nils. In time, he may become one himself.

I climb the cement stairs to the upper floors where the presses blare, echoing in the stairwell.

Every inch of the hall is known to me and freighted with memories. I bounced a ball down these stairs while my father worked. I slid down the metal bannister with Sean when we worked the nightshift, leaving our press clicking through stacks of paper. I stood before the same blank metal door hundreds of times when I came to talk to Nils, to ask his advice, to tell the latest information.

I open the metal door and walk into the office, clean but stark, a cement cell no different from any of the others in the hall. Despite our reverence, Nils never turned lordly. He is one of us. In the corner, broken presses wait for Nils to heal them. Stacks of printed forms line the floor, and Alliance work orders are tacked to the wall. Along the far wall are rows of simple photographs, black-framed and small, hundreds in all. The Martyrs' Wall. My eyes automatically seek out my father. From where I stand, he looks no different than the rest.

Nils sits behind a metal desk, his back to me, texting quickly, graceful fingers recording a secret message, a plan for a new job. He gauges the weight of my footsteps, hears my breathing, senses immediately who it is and why I am here. The unrelenting closeness of the guild links us forever.

'You're supposed to be in Shattuck, aren't you? Freeing Sevenheads' cash from a bank?' His voice is soft and quiet.

'Yes. But something happened.'

'Something's always happening.' Nils turns and smiles at me, eyes shining. I want to hate Nils. I want to blame him for Sean's death, for the innocent martyrs on the wall behind him. But his face is serene, his eyes kind. He looks honest and trustworthy. This is Nils' great strength – the ability to look like he's someone he is not.

I say nothing, waiting for all-knowing Nils to divine the reason I came back.

'Where's Gerry?'

'In Shattuck. Back at the bank.'

'Sean?'

'Culled.' Tears push from my eyes, beyond my control. I wipe them away with the sleeve of my drabs.

'It's terrible,' he says. 'The most terrible thing I can think of.' Nils stands and walks quickly around the desk, pulls me close. I shut my eyes tightly and breathe in his familiar smell of ink, coffee, and oranges. 'But it's over now, Ian.'

'Doesn't feel over to me.'

'But it will be. You'll get better,' he says slowly. 'No matter what happens, I promise that this is the worst of it.'

I pull away. 'Not for Sean. He's still lying on the floor of the vault room with a hole in his head.'

Nils walks to one of the barred windows, scans the streets with a practised efficiency for any potential danger. 'Tell me how it happened.'

'Sean got nervous and started shooting with an ancient gun he found in one of the boxes.'

'So he culled himself?'

'In a way. But Gerry pushed him too far, he scared him with –'

'That's Gerry's way, to push people too far. He doesn't know a different way.' Nils moves a silver tray of dates across this desk toward me. I am so hungry that I can't stop my hand from reaching toward them, from taking one, swallowing the flesh with only the briefest chewing, flooding my mouth with sweetness. I place the smooth pit carefully back on the tray.

'He is not without his faults, of course. But Gerry has served us well.'

I say nothing, take another date, so rare and delicious, sweet as knowledge. But I know now that my father's lesson to me as a boy is true – some knowledge is unalterably bitter.

'Have you found Sevenheads' cash?'

I shake my head. 'He didn't leave it in that bank.'

'You found his box, then?'

'Yes.'

'What was in it?'

'His dead child. The one with seven heads.'

Nils pauses, winces at the news. 'What did it look like?'

I am the teller again, the source of details, sequence of events. 'It turned black and hard.'

'Like?' Nils always wants metaphor to leaven the simple facts.

I think of Gerry for a moment. 'Like a black heart.'

Nils nods, satisfied. 'A frightening thing to encounter in the middle of the night. A black heart. This is what pushed Sean too far, no doubt.'

'Yes,' I say, simplifying.

Nils circles through the room, gazing at the cement floor. He paces to the window again and stands staring out into the grey morning, so slow to brighten. 'You have to go back,' he says. 'You know that, don't you?'

I say nothing, though every fibre, every thought screams

no. I am lucky to escape from the vault room. To go back tempts fate.

Nils senses my hesitation and tries to break down my resistance. 'Sevenheads has left us a message. A ploy. Like a dead man on a pirate's chest. I suspect that his cash is still there in the bank, in another box. He simply wanted to scare us off. And we can't let him.'

'But we found other cash. A bag full of it.'

'But it isn't Sevenheads' cash. Everything they have in Shattuck is something that has been taken away from us. Our work is to get it back, all of it. That's the way you have to think about it.'

'Us and them,' I say flatly.

'Yes.'

'They steal. We steal it back,' I say softly. 'It goes on forever.'

'Exactly. That's the heart of this story. Except in the end, there will only be us.'

'How do you know?'

'Faith,' Nils says. 'I have faith.'

'In what?' I try to disguise the disdain in these words, but cannot.

'In our strength. In our eventual victory. Our survival.'

Nils follows my gaze to the Martyrs' Wall.

'Your father died protecting the guild. You are very much like him.'

'Gerry says he died because Sevenheads was jealous of him.' My father wasn't a hero or a martyr, just culled like any other – a victim of poor timing, petty jealousy, and his own desires.

Nils turns. 'Gerry told you that, did he?'

'Yes.'

'That's an intriguing interpretation.'

'What do you mean?'

Nils pauses and stares at me for a moment, evaluating. My

thoughts wait like rocks at the bottom of clear water, every detail visible to him. I wonder if he can see my dissatisfaction, my plan to leave with Melina.

'Gerry was the one who cast your father out,' Nils says firmly.

I shake my head. 'That's impossible.' But I had never known Nils to lie.

'You've seen Gerry do worse,' Nils says. 'Wouldn't you say he's capable of anything?'

'Anyone is capable of anything,' I say, knowing that it is true.

'Gerry was jealous of your father because he knew so much more. He was like you, someone who remembered everything around him. He could tell the colour of ink from its smell, memorized the screening algorithms. Gerry can't think, can only act. When he's printing, he can't even remember how to mount the plates. He knows very little, and this makes him angry at anyone with any measure of wisdom.'

'But that's no reason to cull my father.' I imagine my father trapped outside the hall as the black wind swept through the city. He choked while Gerry stood inside, breathing in, breathing out, staring out the security portal, eyes darting, lazy mouth working.

'Gerry was trying to prove something to me.'

'What?'

'That he was without conscience. That he could commit cruel acts without a second thought. At that time, it was a very important skill to have.'

'And now?'

Nils shrugs. 'Less so. Times are not quite so desperate. The Chaos is over. Living now is heaven by comparison. You remember, don't you?'

Of course I remember. The guildhall was our fortress against the chaos that played out on the streets below. We cooked rations and nestled in cement rooms like pale, ink-stained night creatures. We breathed oxygen while others choked below. Our language turned inward, our ways arcane. Our litanies grew longer and our songs praised ourselves, claimed that we were chosen, different. And certainly we were different. But not better.

Nils walks around the front of his desk and puts his arm on my shoulder. 'You can accept that terrible things happen in terrible times?'

I say nothing.

'Your father was a martyr. Now Sean is too. Our history is printed in their blood. In the future, others will add their verses, chapters. Perhaps you will join them.'

That I don't share Nils' enthusiasm for martyrdom must be obvious. He pulls away his arm and returns to his desk to busy himself among the papers. 'You know what you have to do, don't you?'

'Go back,' I say softly.

'Of course. Go back,' Nils says. 'This job isn't over. We haven't achieved our goal. You have more work to do.' He looks up for a moment, fingertips poised lightly on his desk, green eyes narrowing. 'Besides, don't you want to see how it all ends?'

I let the last question hover, just turn and walk out of the office and down the narrow stairs to the street.

In the empty square the sensor blinks red, faster now, sending the privileged and fortunate to their shelters. Melina waits just a few minutes away. I hope that she remembers to wear the Special Privileges pin I gave her, that Mrs. Boyle will keep her safe until I come to the settle. The sky verges toward sickly green. A few less oxygen molecules per square metre and the sensor will switch from red to black. *Black, black, you don't come back.*

I run through the West End toward Shattuck, a soldier of lead. Nils was right. I still have work to do.

○ ● ○

In Shattuck Square, a parade struggles on. A row of gas-burners moves slowly down the street, each steered by a proud owner, pushed by gangs of heavy-breathing sunrisers, their drabs marked with sweat. Tons of machinery, chrome, and leather interiors circle around Shattuck Square. In the barren centre beneath the enormous *S*, dozens of other ancient vehicles wait on display, some so tall that the drivers have to climb wooden ladders to get behind the wheel. They are lined up in formations to simulate the Consumption, when the roads were full. The gas-burners can't be started, of course: that's against Alliance policy, punishable by tagging. No unauthorized carbon.

Some walking in the parade wear oxygen masks, others pause every few minutes to sit on the ground and breathe. A scattering of spectators surround the square, shaking their heads at the persistence of fools. The sensor blinks red and the sky turns more ominous by the minute. But no one seems to be hurrying to shelters. We have been lulled by green days, by the rarity of the black wind. The tagged and the scrambled line the square to watch the parade, a rare diversion.

The crows suddenly rise up and fly away from the sagging sign that announces the parade, as if called by a hidden summoner. *A bad sign*, Sean would say. They disappear in the distance, a configuration of dark points travelling across the roiling sky.

The gas-burners coast around the square in a slow circle for a few moments. If I squint my eyes I can see the vehicles, but not the people pushing them. I imagine a time when the city was nonchalant, when actions had no consequences. I daydream of Retail and its endless variety, giving in to it like sleep.

I walk away from the square and down the alley to the sign of the white tooth, passing quickly through the front door and into the dim office. I pause at the raw concrete portal that leads into the bank, remembering Sean drilling it such a short time ago. The exhaustion that I kept hidden at the guildhall comes back in full force. The air is so thin that bright particles drift along the edges of my vision and I have to breathe into my hands for a moment to clear them. Then I climb through the hole and into the bank.

The open door to the vault room waits. I stop for a moment and try to prepare myself. Whatever the end to this story, I am sure it will not be good. Gerry must have left with the duffelbag of cash, since I don't hear anyone working in the room. Will he carry the cash to Nils or set off for a new life, freed from the guild? I can't say. But I know that Sean's cold body will be stiffening on the floor next to the vault room's boxes. I will carry him back to the hall, where we will bury him with the other martyrs in the catacombs beneath the guildhall's foundation.

I step inside slowly, my mind freighted with dread. Gerry lies on the floor next to Sean, his eyes closed. For a moment it seems like he might be culled, but his chest rises and falls in his sleep, his thick fingers move on the shaft of his steel harpoon. The room is strewn with opened boxes, dozens of them, pierced, pulled out, rummaged. My steps rustle dry papers and Gerry opens his eyes slightly, tightens his fingers on his provo stopper.

'I didn't find anything,' he shouts. 'I looked in them all … but I didn't find anything. Even Nils' box was empty.' Gerry's glistening tongue coats every word as he speaks.

'What do you mean?'

'It means that Nils pulled out his cash.' Gerry sits up. 'He didn't trust us.'

'He was just being careful. That's how he is,' I say.

Gerry is alive, thick and moving, an insult to Sean's still body. 'Nils must not have thought I'd be able to pull it off.'

'Maybe he's right,' I say coldly.

'Don't be mad at me, Ian. I'm sick,' Gerry whispers.

'We're all sick. It's a red day.'

'Red, red, you're almost dead.'

'Why did you cull my father, Gerry?' My hands shake and I fight back tears.

He shakes his head slowly. 'I didn't.'

'You're a lying air-waster.'

He pauses. 'Well, I guess you deserve to know, honest-like.' Another long pause. 'Yes, I cast him out one night. But it was an accident.'

'Why? He was your friend.'

'He was smarter. I thought I'd keep him out there for a while, choking, maybe even let him pass out for a minute. Then I'd rush out and rescue him. Nils would be proud. I'd be a hero. He'd respect me. At least that was the plan.'

'What happened?'

Gerry shrugs. 'I fell asleep.'

I drill my gaze into his half-open eyes. 'What?'

'I'd been up working the night shift, running forms. I got tired. I fell asleep and forgot to let your father back in.' He nods. 'That's all there is to the story.'

I say nothing. I spent years puzzling over my father's death. Finally, Gerry's alt version makes it clear. It takes so little to end a life – a misstep in an old minefield, a smug's stopper, ten minutes without oxygen. If I need another reminder of the provo nature of life, I have it.

'You have to forgive me,' Gerry says quietly.

'No, I don't.'

'But I'm sick.' Gerry pulls up his drabs and I can see an enormous growth that stretches his pale skin out in a low sphere. The skin from his grey belly to his chest seems to pulse, darkness showing through the opaque skin, as if Gerry carries his own blackened child within.

I shiver and look away.

'It's been growing for years. Nothing I can do about it. If

one thing doesn't cull you, another does.' Gerry pulls his drabs back down and shuts his eyes again.

We all carry growths with us, lodging along our collarbones, sprinkled along our shoulder-blades, hidden deep inside our body's crimson folds, in our marrow. Cells growing, colonizing, living plush even as they choke us, making us elders at forty. This is where our city's once-famous ambition has gone. Each tumour multiplies like a seething grievance. That Gerry's corruption outpaces ours doesn't surprise me.

The cluttered floor of the vault room swarms before me while Gerry sleeps and Sean lies dead among the papers. Sean was right about this job after all. No good has come from it, but maybe that's the point. Expecting any other outcome is foolish. The corner of the room sparkles and my arms tingle. I realize I'm about to choke.

From Shattuck Square, the siren sends out three quick blasts, then repeats.

I run out of the vault and look through the barred window. The gas-burners still line the square, but the crowd is scattering like rats from fire. The sensor blinks from red to black, vacillating between life and death.

I run back to the vault room and stand for a moment, watching Gerry slip away. I reach out my foot to kick his leg, to wake him, save him. But I stop. Instead, my hand reaches for the metal pike and raises it silently over my head. His mouth is open, weak and waiting. The sight of it starts my daemonmill turning, sending out thoughts of how easy it would be to pierce his terrible mouth with his own harpoon, plunging it into his air-starved brain. I think of the ancient satisfaction. There would be justice, finally. Or would there just be more blood on the floor and another false martyr?

The harpoon turns heavy in my hands and I put it down gently next to Gerry, a footsoldier with no conscience, the best kind. The black wind can take its own revenge on him if it wants.

Our guild's stories play out like the same text printed on different paper. Avenge the fathers. Fight the enemies. Protect interests. Take power and cash.

The bonds that held our cell of three together are dissolving even as I stand close to the two others – Sean, innocent and dead, Gerry, corrupt and dying. Three became Two. Now Two would become One. I walk quietly across the room and shoulder the duffelbag of cash, pick up my bullybar, and rush out the door and down the hall without a last look back. Our outside job for Nils is over.

Lined up along Shattuck Square, the row of abandoned gas-burners shimmers beneath methane lightning. The square is empty except for a gathering of Gnostics, who stand with their arms stretched toward the coryalis. Their eyes are wild and they shout in ecstasy to draw the pure breath of God toward them. Their day of redemption is here, perhaps, but my mind is set on surviving.

I run away as fast as I can, but the duffelbag is heavy and I'm not sure which way to go. No shelter here will admit me – this was not my sector. I have no privileges. I can't go back to the guildhall, no longer my home. I have cast myself out. But where am I supposed to go now? Like many questions, this one is answered for me. Across the square, I see two dark figures approaching, one large, the other smaller, a woman. Both wear drabs and walk quickly toward me, the larger figure moving straight like a hawk with a sparrow fluttering around him.

I turn and run away; something about them seems sickening and familiar. I wish I weren't carrying the dead weight of the full duffelbag. Cash gives off an enticing smell that draws the hungry and venal to it. My stomach drops as I recognize the figures from so long ago – Sevenheads and his bird-wife, her tiny legs blurring to keep up with his long, lumbering stride.

They are so close now that I can see the smiles of predators approaching easy prey. *Stealing from thieves;* they have learned Nils' strategy well. They have been watching us all along, waiting for us to do all the work and come out laden with cash, ripe for culling. Though I am exhausted, fear sends me running down the alley as fast as I can. At Division Street I bend down and force the bullybar beneath a tunnelcover. Dropping the duffelbag in first, I climb in and pull the cover back over as quickly as I can.

Huddled in the darkness at the bottom of the shaft, I stare at the dim points of light filtering through the cover's vents. If I move quickly enough, Sevenheads will stay above ground and pass over my hiding place. I try to slow my breathing, stare up as if I can will away all enemies.

Thick fingers darkened by ink reach into the holes and pull up the heavy cover. The dim light from the failing sky falls on me for a moment, then I run toward the West End.

The first tunnel is large enough that I can crouch as I run, distancing myself from Sevenheads. But dragging the bag behind me along the cement gives out a telltale scraping sound. I throw it on my shoulder, but can't stay low enough to run. My breathing heaves and rasps. Heavy footsteps echo behind me. At the next waystation I climb in a smaller tunnel, little more than a dusty conduit, crawling on my hands and knees, the duffel hooked on my ankle. It's too narrow for Sevenheads to follow, and I imagine that I'm free.

I hear an echo of birdsong behind me and remember his tiny wife.

I crawl faster, the cement grating my palms until I leave a trail of bloody prints glistening on the tunnel behind me. I try to pull my drabs over my hands, but the sleeves are too short. In my nightmare, all I had to do to get away was write low sentences and crawl across them. But nothing I can write will save me now. This is the teller's weakness: words pale next to deeds.

These thoughts fade quickly, overruled by a primitive sector of my brain awakened by fear. I wish for Sean's ancient gun, or a stopper. I have nothing to protect me except my wits. I can crawl faster than my pursuers, find my way more quickly through the familiar tunnels, lit only by narrow shafts of distant light.

Tunnels branch out from a waystation littered with fallen cement. I choose the narrow tube that leads toward Central Station. If I can reach the station, I will be safe. It's a delusion of the endangered, that a familiar place will be safe. I dive into the tunnel with my arms outstretched, as though swimming downstream on raw concrete. The duffelbag barely fits, and drags like an anchor scraping across the harbourfloor.

Behind me my enemies crawl, their thick breathing reverberating in the conduit. Sevenhead's guild is joining the chase, hunting down the foolish West End printer who has strayed into their sector. They are too intent on pursuit to shout out messages or threats.

I am tiring, slowing. My hands slap along the concrete as fast as I can make them, but they are raw and my bruised knees ache. My own panicked breathing echoes in my head and my sides heave beneath my torn, sweat-soaked drabs. I make a decision without thinking; I have no time to think. I pull the duffelbag as close as I can and lie on my back, the cement no more than an inch in front of my eyes. I kick at the duffel as hard as I can, pushing it until it becomes a plug of canvas and lucre. I will leave our hard-won treasure behind, but no one will be able to get past it. I will crawl on, alive, for now. Cash will save me as it promised to save so many others.

I kick hard, pummelling the duffelbag until the clasp bursts open. A gust of crumbling papers sprays out and something soft grazes my cheek. Baby hair. I lie back on the cement, the enemy just a few feet away, and laugh until tears run from the corners of my eyes and trail into my ears. Our outside job for Nils came down to paper and hair clogging a cement tunnel deep beneath Shattuck.

I shake my head at the irony of it all – one that Nils won't share. My story will soon find its way into his litany of those who brought shame to the guild. I have broken the first litany. *Precision above all else.* The lush bag of cash still waits back in the vault room, guarded by two dead guild brothers.

I hear a screech of birdsong just beyond the duffelbag and crawl on, freed from my burden. Cash or worthless paper – it weighs about the same. The howling voices of my pursuers fade in the distance as I come to another waystation and switch to the wider tunnel that leads to Central Station, still miles away, but closer with every stumbling step.

I crawl behind the tangle of wooden benches on the station platform, burrowing deep into their centre where I hid as a child, a boy, and now, as an exhausted fugitive. Above, I can hear the distant sirens and alarms that announce the black wind's progress from sector to sector. There is enough air trapped underground that I can breathe, for a while. I will stay here, hidden, until all danger has passed, then find my way above to Melina.

From where I lie on my back among grey rags and rotting wood, I can see the ceiling's plaster skin peeling away and hanging in spiralling ropes. On the plaster that remains, I can still make out the ancient mural of the West End in another time.

At the top of the mural, I see the familiar figure standing at a window, watching the crowd below. I know his cold gaze well, the look of a dissatisfied father. His hands rest on the windowsill, as if he has just closed the window on the noise and dirt, then stopped to take one last look. I want to turn my back on the world, on Sevenheads and Nils, on the Alliance and the opposition, on everyone except Melina.

For years, I have imagined the story of two lovers who escape the city. It is an invention, of course; a tale no more real than any other. Its setting, *terra voluptatis,* is unbelievable, no more than a sketched-in dreamscape.

I lie beneath the ruins of another time, drifting slowly into sleep as sirens sound and the black wind culls.

The voices echo off the cavernous station. Sevenheads is coming to chase me down and cull me. Or perhaps it is Nils and some apprentices, ready to make an example of the guild brother who has gone astray. Heart pounding, I crawl up carefully through the benches.

A stream of people courses through the station, women in drabs with children at their breasts or clutching the hands of sons and daughters. As they walk slowly down the tracks the children carry limp dolls, threadbare cloth animals. The men push wheelbarrows full of rations and dishes and clothes, valuables torn out of closets and drawers and thrown into something that can be carried or wheeled. They bear with them the tangible sadness of people leaving, forced out by the black wind which sends them underground to trudge through the tunnels like a vast, lost army.

Their eyes search around them, as if some sanctuary might be found in the wrecked station, one of many that would mark their journey away from the city. Perhaps an answer to their unasked question – *Why is this happening?* – might be found scrawled on the tunnel's cement walls or discerned in its crumbling mural. In the grey light their progress seems slow, loss and despair encoded in the ancient rhythm of their feet stepping along the tracks. They walk slowly because they don't want to leave the city, because there are many miles ahead of them before they will be safe, before they will be home again.

Tears flow down my face as I watch the crowd pass, though I know no one, recognize no guild brother or friend. These are people without guilds, cash, or special privileges. They did nothing wrong. They work, survive from day to day, love their wives and husbands and children. They have done nothing to challenge the Alliance or anger God. But they are walking, leaving familiar rooms and settles and streets behind them. I am witnessing the latest in tens of thousands of years of forced marches, evacuations, relocations, tear-stained trails leading west, railcars filled with huddling families. In this cycling repetition I see the boundless cruelty of the world rising up again, intertwined with its infinite love, which will protect them along their journey. I lower myself back down to the station floor, unable to watch.

I don't know how long I slept on the platform – the light stays dim underground. I wake panicked, expecting to find myself in the vault room. Part of me is still lying next to Gerry and Sean. Part of me will always be trapped there.

Melina is safe, protected by Mrs. Boyle and her followers. I tell myself this because I can't face the alternative. I have to find her. We can slip out while the city is still in disarray.

I realize I have nothing with me but what I carry in the pockets of my drabs. It is enough. In the guildhall's echoing rooms I grew up wanting little, expecting nothing. Now, though I carry little with me, my thoughts brighten as I take the first step down the long, straight tunnel toward Mrs. Boyle's settle and Melina. I heed my mother's advice, trusting in hope if only because there is no alternative.

I climb up to the streets, hear no sirens, no crowds. I push the cover up with the bullybar and peer out at the empty alley. Crawling out, I blink like a rat creeping from underground into light. At the end of the alley, I flatten my back against the warm brick wall for a moment, breathe in the city's familiar perfume of woodsmoke, onions, and dust.

The world is locked in silent aftermath. The sensor at the corner blinks yellow. Above, the coryalis glows like an opal, small but sparkling with fire. I pull my drabs around me and stare at the ground, try to stay invisible – impossible, since I am the only walker on this street, perhaps in the entire sector.

Ahead, a transport waits at the corner, metal walls battered and rusted, lights blinking slowly. I step up onto the platform, wondering whether it holds some news about what has happened. When I look inside, I see the answer. All of the riders are sprawled on the floor, faces pressed against the vents. Women hold their children above their heads to catch the last pure air. Men lie, eyes wide open, teeth bared, mouthing final instructions. The driver is next to the door, keys in hand. The black wind culled them all.

I step back and run down the street, seeing now what I didn't notice before. Every low entryway and underpass is thick with drab bodies stacked like sandbags. The black wind reached deep into the sector, stilling a wide swath of the ill-fated, unaffiliated, poor, scrambled. To the Alliance and its supporters, *hyper-evolution* must sound like an intriguing theory. But it looks like slaughter to me.

I run past cornershops, doors swinging in the wind but empty of customers. I race up one street and down another, raising crows from the ground for a moment before they settle again. They have returned to the city to claim the dead, tugging at hair for nests, pecking at shining rings and eyes. Further down the street, eager scavs already attend to the bodies that lie in the street, their crescent knives working away to free jewels and cash from cooling flesh. They look up, eyes narrow and bright with their ancient work, and watch me pass, uninterested in someone who moves and wears nothing of value. I race down the street, searching for Mrs. Boyle's settle.

Mrs. Boyle's street is as silent as the rest, her settle no different from those around it except for the three wavering chalklines on its door, a talisman that I hope has served its purpose and protected all within. I knock, but no opposition apprentice waits to let me in. I pry the door open with the bullybar and run up the stairs.

Mrs. Boyle sits at her desk, pen in hand, still as a statue of an opposition leader. Along the floor, overturned bottles among the sprawled bodies fill the settle with the sickly sweet smell of wine. Mrs. Boyle stares angrily across the room at her colleagues, as if they are simply sodden or exhausted. Her pen didn't save her; it kept her out of the shelter to die among the flawed young men she always favoured. I reach up to touch the black tag on her ear, then move my fingers over her eyes to close them. She will see no more injustice, detect no more conspiracies, fight the Alliance's control no longer. Her anger at *l'armée grise* is finally stilled, a fire extinguished by a wind. Mrs. Boyle lived and died true to her convictions and I know few in the city who can say the same.

I look down at the page she was working, her handwriting growing more scrawled with each sentence. I expect to find some last brilliant illumination coaxed out as the oxygen dwindled and the room turned silent. But the last words on the page are simple. *I'm sorry,* she wrote. That these would be her last words surprises me. Then, in the dim light of the settle, I see that she carefully crossed out the words, knowing better than to expect forgiveness.

I search among the still bodies scattered along the floor, their spirits drifting up to flow through the insatiable coryalis. I find Jason, my press assistant, curled in a corner, face twisted in a final scream. I find others with distended, reddened tongues. But Melina isn't among them. I run upstairs. The texting room is empty. I kneel to smell Melina's familiar scent on the daybed pillow.

Downstairs I search for Melina again, moving aside the strewn bodies roughly, frantically, to see if she lies protected beneath them. In one corner, I find the small pack that contained the mobile press and pick it up. I'm sure there are other more useful things to scav from the opposition's headquarters – rations and cash. But the press seems more important. As I walk downstairs to leave the settle, I shoulder its small burden.

○ ● ○

The all-clear siren blasts and the streets turn alive again. People struggle to carry sacks, wooden crates, trunks. They walk calmly down the street, gold pins shining in their ears. They gaze coldly around them. Having been spared where others perished, their good fortune seems to stun them. That fate was on their side this time offers no assurance that it will be again, though special privileges help shorten the odds.

As I pass through the crowd of the lucky, the spared, I search for Melina's familiar dragging gait, her beautiful crooked smile. As I near the shelter, I see a mass of bodies stretched along the cement, stacked several high, each one with its arms stretching toward the blue steel doors of the shelter. They died, as my father did, struggling to breathe. In death, they form a monument to yearning more terrible than any sculptor could ever summon up.

The doors of the shelter are open now, and each survivor has to step across the bodies of the dead. They walk along the sturdy backs and on soft hands, numb to the horror of it all. No one looks down to acknowledge, cringe, cry.

People stream from the shelter, but Melina isn't among the survivors. Without Mrs. Boyle to guide her, she might have wandered away from the shelter, found herself trapped outside again. I run forward as the crowd thins. A few stragglers emerge from the shelter, those who carry the most. They avoid my gaze, embarrassed by what they carry, or just intent on protecting it – enormous bundles of cash, heavy gold bars wrapped in cloth that does little to disguise them, boxes full of the same debris we freed from the vault room's narrow boxes.

There is a lull at the shelter doors. The survivors are all out now. I stand for a moment wondering where to look next, then turn to run to the next shelter, heart racing.

'Ian.' The small voice sounds pinched and scared. Melina stands at the shelter door, last to leave, unable to walk across the culled. I take her hand.

'They're sleeping,' I whisper.

Melina nods. 'They closed the doors tight to make it quiet, so people could sleep. They knocked for a few minutes, then stopped.' She stares at the mosaic of bodies that lines the square.

'People have been working very hard lately,' I say. 'They're very tired.'

'Mrs. Boyle sent me here. They let me in because of the lucky earring you gave me.' She points to the gold pin glimmering in her ear.

I pull Melina close. 'I'm so glad I found you.'

'Are we going back to Mrs. Boyle's? Is it time to work?' She sees that I am carrying the printing press.

'No. I think the *Sliver* is going to go quiet for a while.'

We pass squads moving down the street, breaking down doors to take away the culled. I wonder if each settle holds the same silent still life that I found in Mrs. Boyle's office. I clench the hand that isn't intertwined with Melina's. Why did the black wind come to this sector? Why not Shattuck, the East End, or Harbourside? Then I recognize these thoughts for what they are, the beginnings of hatred.

They were spared and we weren't.

They have oxygen and we don't.

It could easily have gone the other way. The black wind

enforces an impartiality that the Alliance does its part to control and subvert.

Far ahead, I see smugs stopping all walkers, checking papers. Among them I recognize Keith, my classmate, with his thickened middle and larval eyes. Is he still looking for me? I can only guess that he is.

I point at an abandoned transport, its doors open and waiting. 'I think we'll ride.'

We step up. Melina sees the passengers, sleeping forever.

'Sit here so you don't wake them.' I point next to the driver's seat and Melina huddles quietly on the floor, eyes wide. She is attuned to fear, charts its rise and fall. Perhaps she knows exactly what is going on, but chooses to stay wrapped in her own alt version of this morning. Given the choice, I might do the same.

I reach back and take the keys from the driver's stiff fingers, then put on the official dark blue hat that smells of his sweat.

Melina smiles. 'All passengers remain in their seats,' she intones, mouthing the usual litany of transport drivers. 'Obey city safety regulations. Be prepared to present your identity card before entering or exiting the transport.'

I start the electric motor and scan the controls for a moment.

'Do you know how to drive, Ian? This isn't a printing press, you know.'

I nod. 'Driven them dozens of times.' I move the throttle and the transport moves uncertainly down the tracks. Melina giggles and the passengers sway.

'Next stop, *terra voluptatis*,' she shouts, then raises her hand to steady herself.

The transport picks up speed. We pass squads carrying bodies, people bent in anguish. A fire burns on the outskirts of the sector, flames spilling out of the windows of a brick settle block, but no one is trying to put it out. There are plenty of buildings, more than we need.

The transport drifts through the city as if we are invisible. As we approach the sector border, a red barrier lowers slowly and a smug walks out, palm toward me. His stopper gleams in its black holster.

I press my eyes shut.

'What's wrong, Ian?' Melina whispers.

'Nothing. Just a checkpoint.' I open the door and the smug looks in, sees the bodies. He shakes his head.

'Hundreds culled,' he says. 'That's the word we have.' He looks at my stained drabs, unshaven face, official hat. 'A volunteer, are you?'

'Yes,' I say.

'Off to the incinerator?'

'Yes.' I'm glad this smug is providing the answers I don't have.

'And you know where it is, do you?'

I say nothing.

'Northside, near the frontier.' He steps back and waves me forward.

I carefully take off the brake and move the transport ahead. We pass through sectors untouched by the black wind. Drabs walk down the sidewalks. They stop at cornershops. The sensor is shifting back to green now. *A green day, breathe away.* But just a dozen blocks away, the streets are lined with people who will never breathe again. My eyes cloud as I remember Mrs. Boyle at her desk.

'What's the matter, Ian?'

'I was thinking about Mrs. Boyle.'

'She's sleeping, isn't she?'

'Yes.'

Melina pauses for a moment, frowns. 'She'll see my parents, then. My mother's name is Vanessa. My father is Billy. They died when I was born.'

I say nothing.

'I'll see them again some day. Mrs. Boyle. Her cat. My parents. All the others. There are so many.'

'You will,' I say. 'But not for a while.'

'No, not for a while.' Melina forgets her parents, finds a drab shawl and pulls it around her. 'Will this be a long trip, conductor?'

'Maybe.'

Melina lies down on the floor. I want to be next to her, our bodies close as two kerned letters. 'I'm going to close my eyes for a moment,' she says.

I reach over to pull the shawl over her curled body, then switch the transport's sign to *Out of Service*. We drive slowly ahead, passing unchallenged until we come to the city's edge. To our left, smoke rises from a conical steel incinerator as large as our guildhall. I shiver at the thought of so many people so reduced. Fire sets their souls free. If they chose to swoop down into the city, I wouldn't blame them.

To the right are sets of rails lined with transports; this is the northern terminus. Drivers loll on wooden benches at the station, waiting to begin their runs. I turn away from them, following the rusted track along the back of the station.

The transport loses contact with the grid, slowing, lights flickering off, then stuttering back to life with a shower of sparks. But we keep jolting forward. Melina sleeps, eyes twitching slightly beneath pale lids. Behind her, other sleepers shift, the transport's forward motion pulling them down, sliding them back. Flesh, like water, seeks its own level.

Ahead, the track stretches straight into the unmonitored lands north of the city. I have never been here before. When I was younger we were told it was too dangerous, that enemy factions from the Chaos still lived here. Those who fled the city did so at their own risk. There were barbarians holed up in caves waiting to sweep into the city. The Alliance wanted us to stay in our sectors, near shelters, and – as Mrs. Boyle always pointed out – completely under their control.

Our journey seems less dangerous. We pass the remnants of towns destroyed in the Chaos or abandoned after. Houses overgrown with creeper vines, desolate farms with fallen fences. But the frontier still looks lush. The stunted trees hold new leaves and thick underbrush hides the land's scars. We cross a narrow bridge over a river, muddy and low, but still flowing.

An hour north of the city, I see a man at the far end of a field, not cowering behind a tree, but standing proudly, one hand on a shovel, the other raised in a defiant salute. His beard is long and he wears overalls and a wide-brimmed hat. Even from a distance, I can see that his eyes sparkle with distrust at our faltering transport, moving slowly north. Behind him, smoke drifts from the chimney of a small cabin. This vision is repeated dozens of times along the track with minor variations – a distant figure, a homestead, smoke drifting up, the long stare as we pass.

These pioneers don't worry me. It is comforting to see that there is still life outside the city. But I don't want to stop here.

Every child carries a secret destination fixed in their imagination, the place they will go when they escape. The northlands are mine. During long nights in the guildhall, I read about the silent highlands far from the city. For all I know the land may be changed now, terribly changed. But it will still be our refuge from the guilds, Sevenheads, and the smugs' stoppers. We will be alone.

The rolling hills flatten out and the trees give way to scrub and underbrush. To the right, a range of low mountains rises slowly in formation from green and brown to spiked, snow-covered peaks. To the left, long grassy fields stretch toward a line of hills that marks the western horizon. The coryalis seems to hover behind us, staying close to the city. The sky brightens enough that I can see a rare shadow – that of our transport, rushing along next to the tracks.

We are rising gradually, and occasionally the transport loses power, rolls backwards, and jerks forward fitfully again.

Melina stirs, opens her eyes, smiles. 'It's so beautiful.'

I nod. I can understand why settlers might give up the supposed safety of the city to come to these uncharted lands. There are no sensors here, no warning of the black wind. What good is it to be reminded constantly to be afraid?

'I want to walk in snow,' Melina says quietly.

'What else?'

'To sleep on a bed of pine needles. I read about them once. They smell sweet.'

'What else?'

'To see a star. Just for a moment. It happens, you know. There are breaks in the sky, places where you can see through.'

After years beneath low clouds, open sky makes me nervous, as if we may be drawn up into the heavens, rising on the breath of God. I remember a quote from Horace that I memorized at the academy – *Beneath the vengeful stars of heaven, the works of man are ever vulnerable.* We need no more reminders of our vulnerability. Still, Melina is right. To see the stars would be fine. They are not vengeful, just very far away.

The hills around us converge, the battered transport travelling in the narrow valley between them. We are hours away from the city now, further than either of us has ever been from home. But we feel no pull back; the invisible lodestone of hope draws us north. The long day is ending. By now, Nils has sent my guild brothers to search for me, the teller who had written a tale of deceit. For all he knows, I carry a stolen duffelbag of cash.

Ahead, the tracks end abruptly. I slow and shut off the transport, listening to its cooling engine click for a moment.

Melina looks at me.

'We walk from here,' I say.

'To where?'

'To where we're going.'

'North?'

'Yes,' I say, since there is no other destination. Here my plan thins. All of my supplies – extra rations, drabs, blankets, a tarp – are in the duffelbag I left along a tunnel somewhere deep beneath the city. We can only rely on our wits and luck.

I walk back among the unlucky riders. No doubt the culled carry useful supplies I could scav. Cash. Rations. Extra drabs in case the nights turn cooler. Their pockets hold the valuable and the worthless. But I don't want to plunder any more. I have scaved enough.

We step out, Melina carrying the drab shawl, while I carry only the backpack that holds the small press, too valuable to leave behind. I pull on the official blue hat because it looks right for a journey. I reach back in and put the transport into slow reverse, lock it into place, then step back out quickly. The transport and its still cargo drift silently back to the city. Melina and I watch its progress until it becomes nothing but a black dot along the horizon. Then we turn and begin to walk.

I reach out for Melina's hand, steady her as she walks along the gravel road that continues ahead where the tracks stop. We are free, unencumbered, ready to start a new life here in the northlands, *terra voluptatis* perhaps. It will be a better place than the one we left behind – this is the myth that leads us on, the desire that fuels so many other immigrations. We have cast ourselves out. What will we find at the end of the gravel road?

○ ● ○

The small cave barely holds us both, cupping us inside it like the belly of the letter G. We lie with our feet against the far wall, our heads nearly outside. The night air is cooler here and the drab shawl is wrapped around us both. Melina sleeps but I am beyond sleep, exhausted from the days in the vault, the chase through the tunnels, and the walk north. Instead, I watch the road, expecting to see smugs marching to retrieve two lost citizens. But the road is empty, glazed by the dim light of the coryalis, glowing like a tiny snail crawling around the western horizon.

Already, our journey is full of revelations. On the side of the road, Melina found tiny black berries, sweeter than any we have tasted at the city markets. We drank cold water from a stream. The Alliance would have us believe it was toxic, but it tasted pure, so cold it left our teeth aching. Just as the light began to fade to dusk, we found a cave beneath an overhanging rock shelf, large enough to shelter us both.

I should be worried about the future. We have no rations, no tools or weapons, only a little cash. But I can't allow these worries to find a foothold in my mind. They pass through without leaving a mark. We will survive, not through the ruthless cleverness of Nils and my guild brothers, but through an alt strategy still forming in my mind. We will do little, let the days guide us, give over ambition to faith – though not in man. In thousands of years of civilization, all we have managed to do is fight among ourselves, poison the land, and create the black wind. Behind all these struggles hovers the desire for *more*.

Here in the northlands Melina and I will be content with less, with nothing.

Tired from walking, we end our first day free from the city. As I lie half-asleep, the world seems less mysterious to me. All forces become clear, all motivations known. These are the moments a teller waits for, when the grid of time and place fades to reveal a glimmer of the ancient matrices.

Wherever there is something of value – bronze axes, land, spices, slaves, diamonds, gold, oxygen, cash – others will desire it. They will become enemies, despising us for what we have. Us and them, forever locked in battle. What we lose, they win. What they want, we have. Sevenheads and Nils are just the latest version.

Meanwhile, our time on the land is short, the silence around us eternal. The real battle is to fight these ancient impulses and ignore the tempter's voice that tells us to hate, fear, and cull. In this battle, I will be a soldier of steel.

Melina stirs, moves her hands to my chest to text a message, a dream. In the rhythm of her fingers on my skin, I know that it is a story of us, the two who have journeyed far but still have a long road ahead. Melina, made innocent by the damaging world, will be our compass. I can be found scrambled in the last letters of her name, waiting like the final car in a transport to be pulled forward by her singular power.

'Ian,' she whispers, eyes open.

'Yes.'

Melina smiles and moves forward to wrap her arms around me as she has so many times in provo rooms, on shattered floors of settles in dangerous sectors. Now there is no hurry, no one to hide from. The hollow in the earth holds us. We are alone with the swift sky, empty road, and silent mountains.

Envoi

Nils asked me once to write a story that would forever change those who read it. He was sure that there were passages that could cull their listeners. This tale would attract its readers with the promise of easy entertainment and distraction. It would be of love, adventure, and danger – all the ingredients the teller uses to entice an audience like ants to synth sugar.

But once the readers were drawn in, the words would perform a hidden alchemy. The story would ask questions, turn belief to doubt, confidence to weakness. We would print it in bold type and paste it on walls throughout Shattuck, breaking the will of our enemy without spilling a drop of blood. In the ways of conflict, Nils wanted to be an innovator. As always, he expected too much.

I wish I had such faith and confidence.

Melina and I stumble through the valley, up the rising, narrow path. The underbrush gives way to low, round rocks crusted with lichen. Among the rocks wait clutches of bleached bones, monuments to other ancient passings. Melina leads the way; I turned my ankle wandering through the rocky fields looking for food and finding none. We eat most of our rations. We vie with spiders to lick fetid water from the small pockets between the rocks. Our steps turn slow. Melina leads us on.

My thoughts become scrambled. I write long sentences in my mind, trying to create one that will save us. Certain words take on resonance and I mutter them over and over to keep my worries at bay. My provo plan, forged from daydreams and delusions, is proving too foolish for such an unforgiving world. I have built a house of paper. I am sure that our bones will soon join the others among the barren landscape. Or worse: I will stumble first, leaving Melina alone in this wilderness, abandoning her again as her parents once did.

We walk ahead. The wind blows so hard that we have to bend forward against it, as though we are travelling down a narrow tunnel.

Melina turns to smile at me. 'Almost there,' she says, or perhaps the wind pulls her words away and replaces them with this false message.

I long to be beneath the city, navigating the subterranean world I know so well. In that underground maze, we would be safe. We could pass from station to station, invisible, rising up after curfew to scav rations and water, sinking down at dawn again. Our skin would turn pale, our eyes large and searching, fingers curled and quick to grab. But we would survive, I am sure of it.

Here, all is uncertainty, though Melina senses none of it. She moves ahead, never complaining or doubting as we shuffle north. Almost there. *Terra voluptatis.* I am not the first to create pleasure lands where there is nothing. I am not the first to mistake hope for something more tangible, something green and vital that could be put in our mouths to sustain us.

'I'm a liar!' My shout breaks the silence.

Melina pauses, turns to stare at me. 'You're not a liar, Ian. You're an honest thief – even Mrs. Boyle says so.'

I put my arms around Melina, no more of a patchwork than anyone else. We are all sewn together from the bits and pieces that we are given and those we gather, liars who tell the truth as best we can.

We shiver among the rocks, awakened by the scattered light of dawn, so different from the morning grey of the city. We watch as the light plays over the distant plains, then closer, as sunlight falls on the rocky ground around us. Melina runs to cup it in her shaking hands to drink. When the clouds move and the light drifts, she follows. I smile and walk after her.

My joints ache from cold nights and days of walking. Though Melina says nothing, I know she is hungry and starting to worry. In the night, she cried out for her parents. This morning she asked when we would get to the city, as if this were our destination rather than our starting point.

'It's beautiful,' Melina says. The patch of sunlight at her feet falls on dried sticks, lichens, and leaf skeletons.

I take my father's type magnifier from my pocket and kneel down quickly, before the clouds drift again. The metal rim is dented from years in the pressroom, the glass lens scratched and loose as a failing tooth. Through this same aperture, my father looked at the centres of hollow letters and searched for encroaching ink. I hold it close to the dried leaves nestled in a hollow between the rocks, moving my hand to bring the circle into focus, refining the sunlight from yellow to white. I hold my hand still until a searing pinpoint falls on the leaf.

In a moment, it begins to give off a thin column of white smoke.

Melina kneels. The light is so bright that we can hardly look at it. But we can't look away, either. It holds our gaze like a blazing crystal. The edges blacken and the smoke turns thick. When the leaves burst into flame, I reach down to feed twigs into the fire, stacking them like a small burning house. We have no food, no shelter. But we have fire, the beginning of any world.

Melina huddles close to the growing blaze, fed by the wind. 'It's magic,' she says reverently, palms out.

I turn. 'Yes, it is.' Because to make fire appear on the side of the barren road seems more like magic than the work of my father's type magnifier, more than sunlight and physics. Or perhaps I am simply too exhausted and hungry to know the difference.

○ ● ○

Melina's face turns tired and drawn and she keeps her gaze on the road, now little more than a dirt path that has levelled off but gives no signs of ending. We dream of bread and cake, invent meals that we will share in the pleasure lands, still so elusive. Like all who are lost, I keep expecting something to appear – a house, a town, some sign that others have come this way.

But there is nothing, only the rolling hills around us. No waxen crows circle, no rats crawl through the rocks – I would have trapped one, freed it of fur or feathers, and roasted it on our night fire. Melina and I would have huddled like scavs over its carcass.

'How much longer do we have to walk?' Melina asks.

'A while.'

'How long?' Her gaze darts from side to side, as if she needs a precise answer.

'Hours. Days. Maybe weeks.'

'Mrs. Boyle will be worried.'

'She's proud of us, I'm sure,' I lie.

Melina stop suddenly. 'Why? All we're doing is walking.'

'It's enough,' I say.

'Enough for what?'

'Enough for us.'

Melina starts walking again. 'Of course it is. It's all we can do.'

I can't argue. She is right – all we can do is walk and hope.

The stranger appears on the horizon, running down the narrow trail, paying no attention to the treacherous footing. At first I am sure he is a vision summoned by our hunger and exhaustion. But why would a vision be so clumsy? He runs toward us, falling once, twice, again. Melina stops and presses close to me. Have we come this far, trying to escape the city and its dangers, only to be culled by some desperate settler?

He wears a blue tattered uniform and his face is locked in a fierce expression, eyes wide open, mouth shouting into the wind.

As he comes closer, I shut my eyes and pull Melina close, not wanting to see the stranger who will cull us, not wanting to record these last details. The condition of his teeth. His strength. His vicious pleasure as he attacks us.

'I've been watching you. You came from the city, didn't you?' His shout echoes down the path. We haven't heard voices other than our own for days, and even this simple question puzzles us.

I open my eyes. The stranger stands in the road, watching us eagerly, as if we carry a critical antidote. He is thin, his uniform in disarray. He carries no stopper, no knife that I can see. A single bottle of oxygen pokes from the top of his pack. He sees our empty stares, pulls out a cylinder of water and lets us drink from it, Melina first, eyes pressed tight, then me. I never tasted water so delicious. I find it hard to tear my lips away.

The stranger eyes my transport driver's hat, not so different from his own. 'You're my replacement, then?'

I smile and nod. Yes, I am his replacement.

'I've been asking them for months to send someone new,' he says angrily. 'I was beginning to think they forgot about me, that they were just going to leave me up in that tower forever.'

'Tower?' I say.

'It's just ahead. There are instructions inside.'

I nod again, say nothing. He holds out a shining set of keys and I take them.

'Couldn't stand it any more,' he blurts. 'The waiting. It's

like something's always hanging over my head, ready to drop down from the sky when I don't expect it.'

The Sword of Damocles, I think, though I say nothing.

'I can't sleep. Can't think of anything. You'll see what I mean. You will.'

I nod.

'Or maybe you'll be able to muddle through. I don't care. All I want is to leave. The city, is it still there?'

'Better than ever,' I say.

'Any news?'

'People are sleeping well,' Melina says.

I remember the bodies lined outside the shelters, shiver at the thought.

He stops, puzzled. 'I suppose you're tired too. It's a long trip. Can't say there's much to look at once you get there.' The stranger stares beyond us, along the trail that will lead him down past the pioneers, to the transport tracks and the city that waits at the end of the line. He stands next to us, but he is already gone, clustered among the other citizens in their settles and guildhalls, walking among the cornershops, keeping one eye on the sensor, the index of the city's fear. *Breathe or leave.* He's making his choice and we are making ours.

The stranger says nothing, just walks on, leaving us behind like a widowed fragment of text.

We come to the top of a low hill. Between two distant ranges of peaked mountains, the narrow flatland is dotted by rows of windmills. There are dozens in all, three-bladed giants that slice translucent circles high above the ground. The supports are white and stretch skyward in graceful curves. As we walk closer, we hear the blades whirling in the wind, blowing harder now. To the right of the trail waits the tower the stranger mentioned. Without a word, we walk toward it.

A small lookout circled by a metal walkway caps the tall tower, reached by a long metal ladder that stretches up like an elongated letter *I*. Melina climbs first and I follow, legs shaking, hands slick with fear on the metal rungs. I produce a litany of my complaints. I am hungry. My ankle is sore and throbbing. My pack grows heavier with each step. The ladder seems to stretch on forever. But I am alive. We are alive.

I look out at the rising land, the barren plains in the foreground, the mountains in the distance, unimaginably far away.

We stand on the narrow walkway, and the howling wind pushes us toward the edge. Legs shaking, I unlock the door to the lookout and we step inside. Once I pull the door shut behind us, we are surrounded by a silence so deep and welcome that Melina and I laugh until tears come.

The dishevelled room holds a small table and a narrow bed. Near the window stretches a counter lined with gauges and charts. A long, dented telescope mounted on a tripod points toward the path we walked up. While he watched us, the last windkeeper must have seen that we weren't really his replacements, just ragged citizens. But perhaps he was so ready to leave that he could convince himself of anything.

On the side of the tower facing the windmills, the thick windows are marked with scrawled chalk numbers and arrows. Standing at the window, I can see that each windmill is coded with an identifying number. I page through a ledger open on the counter, a concordance of wind and power. In it, the windkeeper charted each windmill's output for the day. The first entries are precise as a schoolboy's journal, while the last pages hold scrawled words that circle the page like a windmill's blades.

'Look at this.' Melina stands near the small table, then reaches out to grab a half-eaten wooden bowl of rice.

We claw at the rice with our fingers, laughing. We take everything we find on the table and shove it into our mouths.

A hard crust of bread. Stale water from a smudged glass. It is enough.

The bedsheets are coiled on the floor along with splayed books and wadded clothes. The windkeeper appears to have spun off all his possessions like a frantic dervish before he left. It seems remarkable that he remembered to lock the door. And more: that he had found us walking along the trail at the right moment seems miraculous. Though I say nothing to Melina, my faith has been wavering for days, driven out by hunger, fear, and doubt. Now that we are safe and sheltered, it returns.

Melina and I put the room in order, picking up the sheets and stacking the books. In the back, we find a small stove and a closet stacked high with water and rations, but no oxygen. The stranger took the last tank. Among the books on the floor, I find the manual for operating the windmills, read my duties, the necessary adjustments and maintenance. I turn to the front of the book and find that my guild printed it years ago. Perhaps my father was behind the press. Or Sevenheads.

I raise the book and smell the winey black ink, the scent of the guildhall. I wait for nostalgia to bring tears to my eyes, but it doesn't. This windswept tower will be our home now. We will not live in fear – what good would it do us? We will chart the day's progress in wind and power, relayed along a copper cable thick as my arm, snaking down the valley to the city's faltering grid.

Among the last windkeeper's notes, I read about days when the gusts were so strong that the instruments couldn't even record it. Other entries find the black wind at work across the plain, the carbon count recorded in fiercely underlined figures, charted as it passes through the narrow valley. The windkeeper was unnerved by uncertainty. We will get used to it, the same way we acclimatised to other dangers the world sent our way.

○ ● ○

We spend days in the tower, claiming the narrow bed as our own, removing all traces of the windkeeper and the others who lived here before us. Their names are recorded in the ledger – some stayed for years, others just weeks. Assignment to this remote look-out meant a two-year banishment. The windkeepers who came before us violated curfew, fought with smugs, broke the Alliance's rules. Melina and I are serving time in what some might have considered a jail. But to us, it is a provo heaven.

The morning fog is so low that it engulfs the tower, leaving us floating in a grey netherworld. We pull up the metal ladder and lock the door, spend hours rolling in the narrow bed, never separated by more than the thickness of a finger, my hands journeying across Melina's skin to trace the slow line of her pale thighs, to stay between them for hours. After these long afternoons, our backs are marked with fingernail scrapes and toothmarks, desire's red runes. We sleep deeply and dreamlessly. Everything we can hope for is here in our tower.

We venture down on a crisp morning, drawn out by curiosity. The roar of the windmills inspires awe, like being in the shadow of an ancient Aeolian ship. We wander beneath them, necks craning to watch the long blades churning above us. It's easy to imagine that they are not turned by the wind, but circle of their own volition, propelling us into a new land. Melina and I press our hands along the thick cable that runs through the field, its black casing warm and humming beneath our fingers. It courses with the power of air, converted into electricity.

That the city is fuelled by the same wind that it fears seems perverse, but not surprising. Opposites often find themselves intertwined – the disease and the antidote, the lie and the truth, carbon and oxygen, us and them.

We come to a plot where one of the windkeepers dragged away the rocks and carved out a narrow bed. Melina turns to me, puzzled.

'A garden.' I know of them only from books.

She nods and kneels to press her hands deeply into the hard soil, working it with her fingers to break the crust. I found some seeds among our supplies, and now I imagine this small plot thick with melon vines and towering sunflowers. I kneel next to Melina and push my hands into the warm earth. We will live and work here as people have done for centuries, long before the Consumption or Convergence, the Chaos or Control. We will live a life uncoloured by fear.

The black wind may blow at any moment, culling us, turning our garden into a burial plot. It may send the tower tumbling to the ground at night as we sleep in our narrow bed. Alliance smugs could march up the valley to tag us and bring us back to the city in chains. The windkeeper's true replacement might arrive and send us away. Or the pioneers around us could rise up and hang us from our tower.

I keep these fears at bay with inherent faith in the world, despite its ever-surfacing evil.

Melina and I will live together here in the northlands, far from the city. We will draw from the low flame banked within us both – we haven't gone cold. We will grow what we can, learn from the lessons that come our way, welcome others who may drift north. Melina and I will consider each minute a haven, each day a vast, empty page. I will tell our tale as well as I can, walking through the valley between hope and despair. I will scrawl our story across the ledger of the land for strangers to read.

Also by Stona Fitch
Senseless

American economist Eliott Gast is a man who treasures the finest things that life can offer – fine food, a good bottle of wine, beautiful music. Until the day that he is abducted in Europe by a shadowy and extremist anti-globalisation group. Eliott is held hostage for forty days, and each moment of his incarceration is broadcast on the internet. His captors inform him that his eventual release depends on the votes – and donations made to their cause – of the millions of people who are watching this most disturbing of reality shows. As Eliott battles to understand why he has been chosen, he unearths sins both small and large. Over the course of his captivity Eliott is deprived of each of his senses, one by one – deprived of everything except the choice of whether or not to survive.

'Startling in conception and disturbing in what it says about our times.' *JM Coetzee*

'A chilling psychological thriller and a brilliant political fable for our time ... should be situated on the literary map between DeLillo and Coetzee.' *Russell Banks*

'An existential thriller told with brutal clarity and dealing with cruelty, voyeurism, consumerism and globalisation. Brilliantly written with pace, style, confidence and insight, this unbearably tense and truly unforgettable novel will leave a lasting impression.' *Doug Johnstone, The List*

ISBN 978 1 906120 31 3; £8.99 (August 2008)

Visit our website for comprehensive information on all of our books and authors – and for much more:

- browse all Two Ravens Press books by category or by author, and purchase them online, post & packing-free (in the UK, and for a small fee overseas)

- there is a separate page for each book, including summaries, extracts and reviews, and author interviews, biographies and photographs

- read our daily blog about life as a small literary publisher in the middle of nowhere – or the centre of the universe, depending on your perspective – with a few anecdotes about life down on the croft thrown in. Includes regular and irregular columns by guest writers – Two Ravens Press authors and others

- visit our online literary magazine, CORVACEOUS. Each monthly issue brings interviews, articles, criticism, and new works of prose and poetry by a variety of authors, both new and established.

www.tworavenspress.com